THE SEVENTH DATE

CHARLES LEMAR BROWN

Broken
Press

To Kathy Fuss

CHAPTER 1

"Good Lord, Dub Taylor, you peed on me when I was six and then you broke my heart when I was sixteen." Katherine Lynn Williams McClary visibly vibrated as she shouted, "What in the hell makes you think I'd ever agree to go on a date with you?"

Dub Taylor smiled and settled deeper into the worn faux leather chair. In a low husky Oklahoma drawl, he calmly spoke, "Because Katherine you want my land and it's the only way, you'll ever lay hands on it. It's either this or I donate it all to the state as part of the wildlife refuge. Besides I think you just made up that story about me peeing on you."

"I did not you... you, old goat. My sister Vicky was there too." Katherine said through clinched teeth, "and she'll swear to it."

"Seven dates. That's the price. Take it or leave it." Dub's green eyes sparkled as he motioned to the papers on the desk in front of her.

"This seems illegal." Katherine ignored Dub and instead turned to Mason Boyd, Dub's lawyer. Mason was obese and Katherine found him disgusting.

"Mrs. McClary." Mason chewed on the edge of his lip, giving Katherine the impression that he was thinking. He reeked of cigars and sweat. Why Dub had chosen him of all the lawyers in the area was beyond reason, but then nothing Dub had done since returning to Tishomingo could be construed as reasonable in her opinion.

"Yes, Mason." She refused to call him mister and his inability to form a thought had quickly worn her patience thin.

1

"I have been in this profession for over thirty years." His left eye twitched slightly as he spoke.

Katherine fought the urge to stand and smack him hard on the back of the head. It was what she would have done to any of her household appliances that were stupid enough to try her. But then he was not an appliance and if he were, Katherine decided quickly that she would have bought a better brand.

"And while this is not what I would call customary," Mason droned on in a voice that reminded Katherine of the slow methodical squelch of the windmill behind her barn, "it is definitely not illegal. I have had these documents checked with two other attorneys and they agreed that—albeit an odd request— it is completely within the realm of a binding contract."

The lawyer's wind ran out before the end of his last sentence, leaving the final two words barely comprehensible. A bout of coughing he caught in the elbow of his dark brown polyester sports coat followed. When he regained his breath, he pushed the stapled paperwork towards her.

"I will need my lawyer to look over this before I agree to anything." Katherine's chin rose as she reached for the contract.

"Figured as much." Dub half-chuckled.

Katherine's left hand pulled papers in as she turned her gaze on Dub, "Figured, huh? You figured. Ain't seen hide nor hair of you around these parts in what's it been… over forty years? And you been back all of six months. And here you have it all figured out. Well, here is how I figure. I figure you're the same worthless asshole that left. I figure this town will be better off once you leave again. And I figure I'd be willing to pay whatever price you're askin' for in these here papers just to get your sorry ass gone."

Dub met the onslaught head on. Like two old bulls across a pasture fence, he and Katherine's eyes locked. Her nostrils flared. He let a half-smile curl the edge of his lip and refused to look away. When it became apparent to Katherine that the angrier she became the more he seemed to be enjoying their little melee, she blinked and turned her attention back to Mason.

2

"Whatever he's askin' plus three thousand," her eyes narrowed, "and no dates."

"Mrs. McClary," Mason began.

"My name is Katherine!" The force with which the words escaped her shot little droplets of spittle onto the side of Mason's desk, "or Mrs. Williams, but not Mrs. McClary. I haven't gone by that name in years!"

"I am so sorry." Mason raised both hands from where they had rested on the table in what appeared a feeble attempt at shielding his face from the glare that threatened to melt the tongue from his oral cavity, "I did not…"

Before he could finish his thought, Dub rose from his seat. He stood five-foot-eight in his bare feet, today he wore a pair of full-quilled burgundy ostrich boots with a rider's heel. He tapped the edge of the desk three time with the middle knuckle of his left finger, "Call me tomorrow, Mr. Boyd, and let me know if I'm gonna be signing paper for the state of Oklahoma or if Kat here has accepted my proposal." With a final tap, he crossed to the door, retrieved an old, sweat-stained, straw cowboy hat from a peg, and opened the door.

"My name is Katherine!" echoed through the small office as he stepped out onto the sidewalk and pulled the door shut.

"Lord, Almighty," Dub muttered to himself as the door closed behind him, "I sure hope you know what you're doin'."

It was not in his nature to look over his shoulder. Too many bad memories piled on too many poor decisions had left the view in that direction unpleasant to say the least. One last adjustment to settle the Stetson firmly in place and he turned right towards Main Street. He did not stroll or dawdle but neither did he hurry. He moved as if each step, in and of itself, had significant purpose and the rhythm of the heels of his western boots striking the concrete sidewalk produced a cadence that suggested determination.

At the corner of the block, he paused briefly to study the architect of the Chickasaw Bank Museum. He had seen it thousands of times but still found it beautifully amazing. It was one of the few buildings in town to which he had never acclimated. Granite-sided, its Romanesque style seemed out of place against the rest of Main Street, and yet Dub got the impression that it was perfectly content in the location it found itself, not unlike himself.

Knowing Carl would be nearing irritation by now, he turned away from the museum. Two blocks further along, he removed his hat as he stepped through the front entrance of Ole Red. He scanned the room until he spotted Carl seated at a table against the back wall. Carl was lost in the menu. The sight of his friend and the knowledge that Carl already knew every word on the laminated paper in front of him made Dub chuckle to himself as he moved across the room. For the last few months, Thursday at noon found he and Carl visiting over lunch.

"Sorry to keep you waitin'." Dub grinned as he pulled out a chair and sat down.

"No problem. Ain't been here long." Carl laid the menu down, and got straight to the point, "How'd it go?"

"Oh, 'bout the way I expected it would," Dub shrugged as he hung his hat on the chairback next to him. "She cussed me a bit then threw a fit at poor ole Mason."

"But did she agree to the dates?" Carl leaned forward. Standing, Carl at six-one towered over Dub visibly but most of Carl's height was in his long legs. Add to that Carl's tendency to slouch, and when seated together the difference was unnoticeable.

"Got no idea." Dub smiled, "I left her with Mason to work that out."

The drop of Carl's shoulders and his long sigh of disappointment did not escape Dub's notice. Unlike Dub, Carl was not a patient man. He was a man of constant mental motion and once a question arose in his mind, he needed an answer, and needed it yesterday. A retired newspaper editor, it was in his nature to want to be the first to know.

4

"Soon as I know, I'll let you know," Dub caught the attention of a waitress as he spoke, and motioned her over.

"What do you mean, he doesn't want any money?" Katherine's hazel eyes narrowed causing heavy creases to form between her perfectly plucked eyebrows.

"He is not interested in your money," Mason explained for the fourth time, "the agreement is for seven dates. At the end of the seventh date, the house, the two hundred acres, and everything that goes with it, are yours."

"And the hundred and eighty acres I'm currently leasing from the son-of-a-bitch," her nostrils flared, and she brushed a strand of her platinum frosted hair away from her face. "What about those?"

"That depends on you," Mason chewed at his bottom lip before continuing, "If you agree to the terms of the contract, nothing changes with the lease agreement. You will lease it until the contract is fulfilled and then it will simply become yours and you will no longer need to lease."

"And what if I fulfill the contract before the lease is up?" her tone moved from aggravated to business and she allowed the muscles in her face to relax slightly.

"Then Dub, Mr. Taylor, will reimburse you the difference." Mason nodded.

"And if I refuse to be a part of this charade?" Katherine demanded.

"You will be reimbursed the difference and the land will go to the state as part of the wildlife refuge." Mason made a movement Katherine could only construe as a shrug.

"And if I refuse the money and choose to fight it out in court to finish out the lease?" Katherine snarled, the aggravation creeping back into her tone.

"Mrs. Williams," Mason breathed in deeply, held it briefly,

then exhaled slowly, "how much longer do you have on the lease?"

"Thirteen months and twenty-one days." The glow of victory on Katherine's face as a smile spread across it was both gorgeous and eerie, the perfect blending of how beautiful a woman's smile can be and the harsh reality that not all smiles are created equal.

"Mr. Taylor is a very patient man," Mason did his best to match Katherine's smile, "and if that becomes your course of action, he will simply wait until the terms of the lease are finished and *then* the land will be donated to the state."

"Men are such assholes." Katherine stated flatly as the glow faded from her face and a cold hard bitterness moved across her features.

"You may be right." Mason's smile widened, "but that has little bearing on how I intend to do my job."

Her eyes locked on his, Katherine rose from her seat, contract in hand, and said, "I'll have my lawyer look these over and get back to you."

Mason stood and offered his hand over the desk. Katherine looked down at his hand as if it were a fresh pile of cow shit that had dared get to close to her shoes. After a pronounced eyeroll, she maneuvered around the furniture to the door, leaving him standing with his hand frozen above the desk.

He stood like a mannequin following her movement with his eyes until the heavy wooden door slammed shut, then with a hearty chuckle, he dropped the hand and eased back into his chair. The angle of the afternoon sun cast a triangle of light across the far wall. Like a beacon its tip pointed at the side of an old tan filing cabinet.

"Don't mind if I do," Mason said aloud into the room as he stood and fished a key from the top drawer of his desk.

He navigated as quickly as his stature allowed around the furniture, unlocked the cabinet, opened the second drawer from the top, and removed a bottle of Gentleman Jack. The clock on the wall above him indicated it was eight minutes past one.

6

"It's five o'clock somewhere," he grinned as he reached back into the drawer for a tumbler.

By the time the minute hand found its way to the bottom of the clock, Mason had finished his first drink and was pouring himself another. "Think maybe I undercharged for this one," He muttered to himself as he placed the top back on the bottle of bourbon.

CHAPTER 2

"Momma! Hey, momma!" Jenn McClary shouted as she glanced into the sitting room and then started down the hall of her mother's expansive country home, "Momma where the hell are ya?"

She passed the doors to a coat closet on one side and the guest bathroom on the other. The door to her mother's room was ajar. She pushed it open without a second thought and stepped in. The king-size bed was made up, nothing unusual there, Jenn had been taught at an early age that one did not leave their room in the morning until their bed was properly put together.

Where the hell is she? Jenn wondered as she passed her mother's antique walnut vanity on her way across the room. She paused long enough to glance at herself in the mirror. At an even one-fifty, she was heavier than her mother by fifteen pounds. Thank goodness she had gotten a little added height from her dad's genetics. She was fond of reminding her mother that at five-six she was a full two inches taller than her. Height and weight, there the differences ended. The reflection staring back at her verified without a doubt that she was her mother's daughter.

The vanity reminded her of her father. Of all the furniture in the house that single piece had nearly been the death of the poor man. Momma had dragged him through every antique store in southern Oklahoma and northern Texas in a search for one that would fit perfectly with the rest of the décor in the room.

The door that led to her mother's private bathing and dressing area was closed. Jenn tapped twice before turning the handle. "Mom, you in here?"

After a quick search of the bathroom and huge walk-in closet, she made her way back to the front foyer. At the stairs leading to the second floor, she paused and stared up at the balcony. Her mother seldom ever bothered with the upstairs, there was enough for her to do on the ground level. Jenn found herself wondering how long it took the crew that came once a week to clean the house to get it all done.

As she passed through the archway that led to the breakfast nook, formal dining room, kitchen, den, and game room, she heard a muffled noise overhead. A quick turn and she was back in the foyer, "Mom, you up there?" she shouted into the empty vault above the front entry.

A door slammed and Katherine's head appeared over the railing, "Good Lord, child, yes I'm up here," she stared down at her daughter. "What in the hell are you yellin' for? And why are you here?"

"Goodness, Momma," Jenn stuck her bottom lip out. "Cain't a girl just decide to visit the woman who birthed her?"

"Jennifer Lynn, you know damn well you can visit me anytime you want to," Katherine scolded, "but you always come on Sunday. You hardly ever visit in the middle of the week."

"Mom, it's Friday," Jenn pulled her lip back in, "hardly the middle of the week."

"Still doesn't answer the question of why you're here." Katherine pursed her lips and cocked her head to one side.

Instead of clarifying, Jenn changed tactics, "What are you doin' upstairs?"

With a roll of her eyes, Katherine moved to the stairs and answered as she descended, "I was up here making sure the cleaners did their jobs correctly and had to use the restroom. I was in the process of wiping my ass when you came bellowing through the front door like a bull in a China closet, if you must know."

Jenn giggled and shook her finger at her mother as Katherine stepped down from the final stair, "You ain't foolin' no one.

You've got a man up there, don'tcha?" She made a clicking sound and pointed at the darkness above.

"Oh, holy hell," Katherine shook her head and shouldered past her daughter, headed for the sitting room, "I don't know what gets into you child. You know damn well I don't have *a* man up there."

"Oh, so you don't have *a* man up there?" Jenn fell in behind her mother. "Just how many men do you have up there, then?"

Katherine ignored the comment and settled down onto one end of a beige couch, picked up a western-style cowhide throw pillow, and nestled it in her lap. Jenn considered taking the other end of the couch but instead dropped into the armchair across from her mother.

"So how many men are up there?" she chided. "There's four rooms. You got a man in each of them?"

"Dammit to hell, Jennifer." The anger in her voice became visible when Katherine reddened.

"One of them won't be Dub Taylor, now, would it?" Jenn grinned.

"Like hell," the words shot forth as a high-pitched squeal, "Dub Taylor can kiss my ass. And you… you're here to pick my brain." She shook a finger at her daughter.

"Correctamundo." Jenn scooched forward to the edge of her chair and waited.

The sound of the pendulum on the big grandfather clock in the corner filled the room. Somewhere outside a horse neighed loudly. Katherine fussed with the pillow in her lap. When it became apparent that her mother was not going to give up information willingly, Jenn sat back in her chair and crossed her legs at the knees.

"He is kinda cute for an old man." She said as she watched her mother for any reaction.

There was none.

"There's talk all over town that you two are gonna date." Jenn kept her tone as matter-of-fact as possible.

Still nothing.

"So, I was wondering," she scrunched her eyes up as if she was concentrating hard. "I was wondering, if things work out, should I call him Dub or Daddo?"

Katherine's head raised slightly and in a calm, business-like manner she said, "Neither, because things are not going to work out. I do not like that man. I would even go as far as to say I despise him."

"You were at Mr. Boyd's office with him on Tuesday." Jenn raised her head in mockery.

"Indeed, I was." Katherine blinked, "I was there on business. My business."

"So are ya or ain't ya gonna take Mr. Taylor's offer?" Jenn asked.

"Wouldn't you like to know?" Katherine's smile held no humor.

Dub Taylor stared at the boxes stacked on the kitchen table. It was a good table, solid, durable, made of some hardwood, oak perhaps, he thought. Six chairs, chipped and scarred to match the table, were arranged around it. He pulled one out and sat. Train up a child in the way he should go: and when he is old, he will not depart from it.

The verse came as his eyes moved from one empty seat to another. The place his father had sat he had always considered the head of the table. Growing up, he had never thought much about the seating arrangements. Dad sat at the head. To one side of dad sat mom and to the other side Ben. And beside Ben, himself. Now the others were all gone. The house was empty and he could choose any seat he wanted. And still he chose the one that had been allotted him in his youth.

The thought brought a momentary smile to his face. A look at the boxes and it faded quickly. Eight in total, they held everything he had avoided in life. Once they had been the home of his mother's shoes, back before his dad had finally agreed to build her shelves to keep them from cluttering up the closet floor. The boxes were old and dusty. The lids could be lifted away unlike the newer ones he had encountered that folded back.

Just think of it as another mission, marine, a deep commanding voice from somewhere in his past sounded off in the recesses of his mind. Master Sergeant Frye, casualty of the Gulf War. Dub had not thought of him in years.

"Not my kind of mission, Sarge." Dub responded aloud.

Still, there ain't no sense in pussyfooting around it, soldier. Open the boxes and set to.

Dub continued to stare at the boxes. Two stacks of four, eight psychological landmines and it was his job to open them up. A strip of curled yellowed masking tape threatened to fall off the end of each of the boxes. Still legible on each his mother handwriting where she had printed the years. BEFORE 1960, that label held no fear for him. The next one — 60 TO 64 — there is where the trouble would begin, he decided.

He took down the first box, removed the lid and placed it to one side, reached in, and took out the first photograph. It was a black and white print of his mother in her wedding dress. Even though it was faded and had a scratch in the bottom left corner, Dub could see the sparkle in her eyes. That infectious happiness that was so much a part of her, the simple act of her entering a room made it feel like everything was right. Then the accident took that part of her away and Dub never saw it again.

The buzz of his cellphone indicated a call. He laid the photograph on the table, rose from his chair, and made his way into the living room. It stopped buzzing well before he retrieved it from the end table beside his recliner. A quick swipe and a couple taps on the screen and he placed it to his ear.

"Mr. Taylor?" Mason Boyd sounded out of breath on the other end.

"Yes, sir." Dub knew his name had flashed across Mason's

screen before he answered the phone and had to smile. The verse from Proverbs popped into his head once again. Old habits, whether good or bad, just seemed to stay with a person.

"I'm sorry to bother you on the weekend." Mason took a deep breath.

"No bother," Dub assured him, "What's up?"

"Mr. Taylor," Mason wheezed before continuing, "Mrs. McClary, I mean Mrs. Williams. I guess that's what we should call her, huh?"

It took a second for the question to register but when it did, Dub chuckled, "Yeah, you probably ought to address her as Mrs. Williams, Mason. I on the other hand, well, I think I'll call her Kat since it seemed to piss her off."

An audible sigh followed before Mason said, "Well, Mrs. Williams has consulted with her lawyer and is ready to meet with us again."

"You don't say." Dub stared out the window at the fence line a quarter of a mile away. Seven strands of barbed wire stretched between old orange t-posts separated Kat's land from his two hundred acres. "Is she acceptin' the offer then?"

"That I don't know," Mason answered. "She just said she was ready to meet. Is Monday at my office at one-thirty good for you?"

"Yes, sir." Dub said. "One-thirty Monday works just fine for me."

"Wonderful, I'll see you then." And then silence.

Dub returned the phone to its place beside the television remote and returned to the dining room. He stared down at the photograph of his mother and contemplated whether he wanted to continue sorting the pictures in the box. He decided he did not. With care, he replaced the lid back on the box, then pushed in his chair.

Staring down at his mother's image, he spoke aloud, "I wonder what she decided."

CHAPTER 3

"Anything I say on the matter would be pure speculation." Dub reached for his cup of coffee as he spoke. "I won't know anything until this afternoon."

"But what do you think she'll do?" Carl's eyes darted around the burger shop scanning for eavesdroppers.

"Now Carl," Kenneth raised a hand, "you're just gonna have to learn some patience. Dub don't know nothing. Hell, knowin' Katherine, she might not even have decided for sure herself."

"Oh, so, you know Katherine do ya?" Carl's impatience was making him irritable.

"I didn't say that." Kenneth was an old, retired dairy farmer with the patience of Job. He was an inch taller than Dub but lean and thin from years of milking cows. Dub figured he would weigh in at least twenty pounds under his own one-eighty.

Carl turned back to Dub, "What are you grinnin' at?" he asked when he noticed Dub's smirk.

"Just enjoyin' the banter." Dub sat his cup back on the table. "Either of you ever realize how little us men really know about the ways of women?"

Neither man offered an answer or an opinion and for several minutes the three simply sat quietly sipping their coffee. Carl folded and unfolded a napkin. Dub watched his hands press each crease as he folded it in fourths and then into a triangle. As Carl began to unfold it for the third time, Dub looked to Kenneth who sat stirring his now lukewarm coffee with a little red plastic straw. Three men drawn together by their morning routine. If not good friends, they were at least more than acquaintances.

"Cows." Kenneth broke the silence, "Cows I can understand. Cows I can explain to ya. Women not so much. Been married for nearly forty years now and most days I feel like I know less about the ways of women than I did the day I said I do."

Dub smiled. "How 'bout you, Carl? How long you been married?"

Carl laid the napkin aside, and looked first to Kenneth then at Dub, "Thirty-eight long years come May twenty-seventh, but who's countin'. And just so you know, I don't know shit about cows or women."

Katherine leaned forward on her settee and checked for makeup lines one last time in the vanity mirror. By her calculations it had been six years since the last time a man had seen her without her face on and her hair fixed. The thought of her ex-husband did nothing at all to help her already sour mood.

She wiggled the bathrobe she wore up over her shoulders, rose from her seat, and pulled the belt tight. She did not study herself in the mirror. She was all too aware of how her appearance had changed over the years. That there were millions of women thirty years younger than her who would kill for her figure was of little consolation to her. She did what she could to reduce the advances of aging and mourned her youth.

Her thoughts turned to Dub Taylor as she made her way through the bathroom and into her closet. She started to scold herself for thinking about him, but then thought, *what the hell I'm already in a pissy mood.*

She could not remember a time when her family and his had not shared a fence line. It had never occurred to her to find out which family moved into the area first, she had always assumed it was hers. Now she could not help but wonder.

From the time she could walk, she and her sister, Vicky, had romped and roamed across both parcels of their family's land.

Back then, the two had nearly the same amount of acreage. It was not until after oil was struck on her grandfather's land in Texas that her own father had begun to expand their little ranch into what it was today.

After the accident, Dub left, and she had not seen him again until he had stopped his truck in the middle of the road four months ago. She had turned from the mailbox ready to give someone a piece of her mind but the sight of him sitting there smiling had shocked her so badly she could only stare.

"Looks like we're neighbors again." He had smiled.

Unable to speak and realizing she must look a mess after having just jogged from the house to the road, she turned without saying a word and started back down the paved lane that led to her house. She did not look back. When she heard the truck turn off onto his gravel drive, she broke into a jog.

Even now as she removed the robe and tried to decide what she would wear, she could feel the edge of her old love for him trying to crowd out the years of hatred and disdain she had so carefully cultivated after he had simply left. *I'll be damned if I let him get to me again*, she thought and pulled a caramel-colored pantsuit from its hanger. A classic white button-front blouse and a pair of heels a shade darker than her suit completed her ensemble.

Once dressed, she returned to the vanity mirror long enough to touch up her hair. Retrieving her Louis Vuitton clutch and key fob, she navigated through the house to the garage. She opened the interior door, pressed the button to raise the overhead behind her Cadillac, and took a deep breath.

"I absolutely hate you, Dub Taylor." She said aloud as she stepped into the garage and pulled the door shut behind her.

"My lawyer assures me that everything in this contract is legal," Katherine sat slightly sideways in her chair with her back to Dub and spoke to Mason, "he further guarantees me that there are no loopholes built in that could be used if I do indeed decide to agree to this contract."

"I see," Mason nodded, "do you have any questions for me?"

"Oh, I have lots of questions," Katherine laid the legal document on his desk, "and I guarantee you if you try to screw me, I'll nail your ass to the wall."

Mason looked from the contract to Dub. How the man could maintain such a cool calm demeanor in such a stressful situation was beyond him. He had helped clients through divorces that were so bad, he had not been sure one of the two parties was not going to murder the other. He remembered one land dispute between two cousins that had come to blows. But in all his years as an attorney, he had never seen a person with as much pure unadulterated hatred from another person as Katherine had for Dub.

"Perhaps we should begin today by trying to answer your questions." Mason suggested.

Katherine opened the clutch in her lap, reached in, and pulled out her cellphone. After a couple of taps on the screen, she squinted at it momentarily before pulling out a pair of reading glasses. Placing them near the end of her nose, she looked over the top of them at Mason. The message was clear, say something about my age or eyes and all hell is going to break loose. Maintaining his best poker face, Mason continued to look at the phone in her hand as if he had not even noticed the glasses.

"First," Katherine looked back to the screen, "what exactly does one of these dates entail?"

"That's a reasonable question." Mason said and looked from Katherine to Dub.

Dub sat staring at the back of Katherine's head. When Mason realized he was waiting for her to acknowledge his presence, and that Katherine had no intention of doing so, he cleared his throat. "Mr. Taylor."

With a grin, Dub turned his gaze to the lawyer. "Well, I reckon a meal or two, perhaps a movie or maybe we could go dancin'."

From the corner of his eye, Mason caught the slight movement as Katherine flinched at the word dancin'. By the time he turned back to her, whatever had triggered it, she had under control.

With another check of her list, she looked up at Mason and asked, "On what day of the week and how often would these dates occur?"

Mason nodded and turned to Dub. Once again, Dub's gaze was on Katherine. *Lord, help me*, he thought, as he spoke, "Mr. Taylor."

"Oh, well now… I cain't say as I've really thought that far ahead." Dub ignored Mason's attempt at drawing his attention towards the lawyer and instead made conversation with the back of Katherine's head. "For the sake of argument…" Dub made a clicking sound, "let's say once every week or so. That sound about right to you, Kat?"

Goodness gracious, man, do you want her to accept this deal or not? Mason thought, as Katherine visible tensed at the name.

Another few seconds and a swipe upwards on the phone, and Katherine looked at Mason once again, "And just so we're clear, no physical… um, no activity that require… um…"

"Don't worry," Dub's grin widened, "I ain't tryin' to get into your pants, Kat. No sex, but if you're so inclined, I might let you hold my hand."

Mason watched as the hand Katherine was holding her phone in tightened until her knuckles turned white. Two hundred acres was a drop in the bucket compared to this woman's holdings. He had no idea why she was so dead set on having it, but he was beginning to wonder just how far Dub could push her before she told him to take a flying leap off the old well house.

"Any further questions?" Mason looked at the filing cabinet behind them. The thought that he was going to need a glass of bourbon when this meeting was over entered his mind as he waited for Katherine's answer.

"Not at the moment," she managed after composing herself, "but I would like one additional provision added to this contract."

"And what would that be?" Mason asked as he pulled the draft across the table and turned it towards himself.

"After each date, we meet back here," Katherine paused while she removed her reading glasses and placed them along with her phone back into her clutch, "just in case I feel the need to make additional stipulations for the next date."

"Sounds reasonable," Mason muttered as he turned to Dub. *These two are going to be the death of me*, crossed his mind as he waited for Dub's response.

"I'm fine with that," Dub shrugged, still looking at the back of Katherine's head.

"Could you do that now?" Katherine asked as she turned forward in her seat. "I'd like to be done with the paperwork before I leave here."

Mason picked up the draft. "Give me five minutes." he said and turned to his computer. In his peripheral he could see Katherine as he worked. Never once did she turn her gaze toward Dub, and while Dub was not in line of sight, he was pretty sure Dub had not yet turned his gaze away from her.

A last key stroke and the printer whirled to life. Dub leaned forward and printed, signed, and dated on the lines indicated. When he had finished, he pushed the document across the desk to Katherine.

"So, should we shake on it?" Dub smiled.

"Just give me a damn pen before I change my mind," she said and met his gaze with a chilling glare.

CHAPTER 4

"How long since you been on a date, Mom?" Jenn asked when Katherine opened the front door.

"No, hi, Mom? No how are you, Mom?" Katherine shrugged as Jenn stepped into the foyer. "Just right to the point. And once again, you show up in the middle of the week."

Jenn did not bother to stop in the entryway but instead continued into the sitting room, leaving her mother little choice but to follow. As she settled down on the end of the couch, she looked up at Katherine. "Hi, Mom. How are you, Mom? Have you lost your mind, Mom? And you're right about the middle of the week this time, Mom. It is Wednesday."

Katherine stood beside the recliner facing her daughter with her arms crossed across her chest. "Hello, daughter. I'm doing well. No, I have not lost my mind. And is there another reason you're here besides to interrogate me?"

"Nope, not really." Jenn raised an eyebrow. "Word down at the shop is that you've agreed to date Dub Taylor for some unknown reason. And for something classified as unknown, there seems to be no end to the speculations that are crawlin' 'round the proverbial grapevine."

"It really isn't anyone's business, now, is it?" Katherine could feel the ire rising from under the collar of her blouse.

"You right, Momma. It really isn't anyone's business," Jenn did a little head wobble, "but we live in small town U.S.A., so guess what: everyone makes it their business."

"Let'em." Katherine's tone was hard and flat. She did not

like to see anyone bob their head from side to side when they spoke, and she hated it when either of her daughters did it. To her it was low-class and reminded her of the old bobble-head figurines she used to see in Lafitte's Pharmacy.

"That's all well and good for you to say," Jenn's head continued to oscillate, "you're hid out here in your little hidey-hole, Little Miss Hermit. But me... me, well, I'm smack dab in the middle of it all. As a matter of fact, one might say my salon is the very root of the town's grapevine."

"So, this little visit isn't really about me then, is it?" Katherine's head tilted to one side. She unfolded her arms from across her chest, clasped her hands together, and fixed her face into her best impersonation of a pouty look. "It's about you and how your crazy old momma has embarrassed you in front of the townfolk."

Jenn's eyes narrowed. "I hate havin' to find out about what's goin' on with my own family from my customers. You could have at least given me a heads up."

"Alright, Little Missy," Katherine placed her hands on her hips and asked, "What would you like to know?"

"Is it true?" Jenn asked.

"It is." Katherine answered.

"Why?" Jenn's brow scrunched. Katherine thought she saw concern on her daughter's face.

"It's the only way for me to get his land," Katherine explained and instantly realized how odd it sounded.

As Jenn's eyes widened in shock, Katherine quickly tried to explain, "He was going to donate his land to the state as part of the refuge. I wanted the land, so I made him an offer. He said the only way I would ever get the land was if I went on dates with him."

Yeah, that really cleared things up. No red flags popping up here. Katherine thought as she watched the concern in her daughter's face deepen.

"Goodness," Katherine sat down on the edge of the recliner, put her elbows on her knees, and leaned towards Jenn. "Now that

I've said it out loud, it does sound a little crazy, but really, Jenn, it's not what it looks like."

"Oh, really?" Jenn did not look convinced.

"Really." Katherine nodded. "It's just seven innocent dates and then I never have to see him again."

"You do realize this sounds like the beginning of a bad stalker movie?" Jenn reached out and placed a hand on her mother's hand. "Besides the dates, how much money is he askin' for?"

"None." Katherine shrugged and attempted a weak smile.

"Seriously?" Jenn removed her hand. "Two hundred acres. Seven dates. No money. What's the catch?"

"There's not one as far as I can tell." Katherine could feel the wheels turning inside her head. *Are you trying to convince Jenn or yourself,* she wondered.

Katherine sat back in the recliner and Jenn leaned into the corner of the couch. For the next several minutes the two sat silent. Katherine, for the first time since it had all begun, found herself questioning Dub's motives. Did he hope to win her heart? Was this his way of apologizing for the past? So many years had passed since they were high school sweethearts. Was he trying to rekindle the flame?

"How long has it been since you went on a date?" Jenn broke the silence.

Katherine took a minute before admitting, "The last date I went on was with your dad the night he told me he wanted a divorce."

"That doesn't count," Jenn shook her head. "I mean on a date-date. An unmarried date."

"I only ever dated two people like that," Katherine admitted after another minute, "Dub once and then your dad."

Katherine watched the expression on her daughter's face go through a series of changes before Jenn finally spoke again. "So, nearly forty years. And you dated Dub Taylor before? Good Lord, Mom, how come I didn't know about this?"

"It was a long time ago," Katherine said, "and it really wasn't a big deal."

"Maybe not to you, but you just wait until folks around town learn about it," Jenn gave her a knowing smile, "I can see the headlines now. 'Old flame comes back to town, sweeps bitter divorcee off her feet.' Damn, Mom, it's the kinda stuff movies are made of."

Katherine scoffed, "Horror movies, maybe."

Jenn ignored the comment, "So forty years, give or take, since your last date. A little over six years since you and dad divorced."

"Yes, and yes," Katherine nodded twice, "but I think I'll be okay. It's just a few dates."

"Just a few dates, huh?" Jenn's calm, serious demeanor caught Katherine a bit off guard. "Mom, when's the last time a man saw your hoochie choochie?"

Katherine almost choked before she was able to respond, "Lord have mercy, Jennifer Lynn, what the hell is wrong with you? Nobody is going to see my... my goodness, we will not be discussing my hoochie choochie."

The additional attention that was being paid to the table was not lost on Dub as he sat with Carl and waited for Kenneth to arrive. The size of the coffee crowd at the burger shop had steadily grown each morning following Katherine's signing of the contract on Monday. Now it was Thursday, and the town was abuzz with the news. Rumor on top of gossip sprinkled with speculation and topped with a cherry was drawing more interest than the coffee cooling in the Styrofoam cups in front of the old men gathered at the tables and booths.

The front door swung open. A momentary hush filled the restaurant as heads turned to look at the new arrival. Kenneth stepped through the door, reddened slightly at the unwanted attention, scanned the room, and made his way to the table where

Dub and Carl waited. By the time he was halfway across the room, the hum of conversations filled the air once more.

"How's Kenneth this mornin'?" Dub asked as he slid across the seat and made room for Kenneth to sit.

"Can't complain," Kenneth's customary response brought a smile to Dub's face. "No one would listen anyway. How 'bout y'all?"

"I'm good," Dub smiled then nodded at Carl. "And as far as I can tell Carl here is his normal cheery self."

Carl rolled his eyes before removing his glasses and reaching for a napkin. "Dub here was just avoiding answering my question," he said as he wrapped the napkin around one lens and then the other, cleaning each of them in turn.

"What question was that?" Kenneth asked.

Carl placed his glasses back on his face. "I was just asking him when he planned to take Katherine on the first date."

"I reckon that's his business." Kenneth offered his opinion as a waitress placed a cup of coffee on the table in front of him and asked Dub and Carl if they wanted their cups freshened up. Dub slid his cup across the table towards her, but Carl declined with a wave of his hand.

As the waitress retreated towards the kitchen, Kenneth pushed Dub's cup back towards him, "Whatcha plannin' to do after this business is all said and done?"

Dub blew across the top of his coffee cup, enjoying the nutty smell. Although not really an earthy aroma, it brought the memory of his father turning his mother's garden. He figured it was because it reminded him of his mother standing in the door with a cup of coffee watching his father on their old tractor getting her little plot ready.

"I think I'll leave that in the Lord's hands." Dub smiled.

Carl snorted. "See what I mean, he's just full of ambiguous answers this mornin'.

"Never meant to confuse ya, Carl," Dub chuckled.

"More like irritate," Carl tapped the edge of his cup. "If

you're so set on keeping it a secret, at least tell us where you're gonna take her."

"Well, I think..." Dub stopped when he realized everybody in the place, with the exception of Kenneth, was looking at him. He smiled as he continued, "I think it would be wrong to ruin the surprise."

"What surprise?" Kenneth wondered aloud.

The anticipation in the room could have been cut with a knife. Dub rubbed a hand across his chin. "The where and when surprise. If I tell you where or when, by noon someone in this room will tell their wife, and thirty minutes later the ladies down at the beauty salon will be telling her daughter, and then... well, you can see how that would ruin the surprise."

By late afternoon on Saturday, Katherine was about ready to pull her hair out. Patience was not one of her virtues and she knew it. Wednesday's visit with Jenn had left her mind in a whirl. She had spent most of Thursday reassuring herself that dating was like riding a bicycle. Then while getting ready for bed that night she remembered she had not ridden a bike in thirty some-odd years and the last time she had ridden, she had ended up with a skinned elbow and a knot on her forehead.

Friday the cleaning crew had arrived and taken the brunt of her frustration. With nothing else to occupy her time, she had roamed the house pointing out what needed to be done like it was their first time on the property. When they left, she called in her grocery order, adding a bottle of blackberry wine to the list. She could not remember the last time she had drank alcohol of any kind, but figured, what the hell. If the town folks were already speculating about her sanity, she might as well fuel the fire.

Seated in a padded lounge, she stared past the pool at the land. The long-stemmed wine glass was empty and for some reason she found that irritating. As she considered whether or not she should make a trip back inside and fill it once more, she suddenly wished she had required Dub as part of the agreement to give her exact dates and times right up front. Now that she had agreed to the dates, she found the waiting more excruciating than the thought of going on them had been in the first place.

Frustrated, she stood and made her way back into the house. In the kitchen, she placed her phone on the marble countertop and carried her empty glass to the refrigerator. She wondered if fulfilling the terms of this contract was going to drive her to drinking, and decided that if it did, she would invest in one of those fancy little wine coolers that looked like a mini-fridge and sat on the counter.

Her glass refilled, she started back outside but stopped when her phone buzzed indicating an incoming call. The number on the screen was local but not one she recognized. She tapped the accept button anyway.

"Hello." She said after pressing the speaker icon.

"Good afternoon, Kat," Dub's voice rang through the kitchen. "Are you ready for our first date?"

Flustered, she stammered, "I'm… I'm…"

"Sorry," Dub chuckled, "I didn't mean to startle ya."

Regaining her composure, Katherine glared at the phone, "You did not startle me. I did not recognize the number that's all."

"Well, I guess you'll just have to add me to your contacts, so that doesn't happen again," he suggested.

Infuriated by the humor in his voice, Katherine snapped, "Fat chance."

Dub ignored her remark. "Tomorrow evening, let's say six o'clock. That sound good to you?"

"Tomorrow is Sunday." Katherine spoke more to herself than to him.

"It sure is, and the day after that is Monday," Dub joked, "So, is tomorrow good for you?"

Katherine shrugged then felt foolish knowing he could not see her and said, "I guess so. Where are we going?"

"On our first date," Dub answered.

"Dammit, Dub, you know what I mean." She reddened. "Where are you taking me on this date?"

"It's a surprise." Even without being able to see his face, she could feel his smile, and wanted nothing more than to end the call.

Instead, with effort she maintained a level voice, "Alright then, what should I wear?"

"I don't care. Whatever you want to wear."

"That doesn't help," she said through clinched teeth. "What are you going to wear?

After a second in which she thought he was deciding on his attire, he responded, "Clothes. I'm gonna wear clothes. I suggest you do likewise. See you tomorrow." And the line disconnected.

She slammed her palm down on the counter beside the phone with enough force to make her hand sting. After glaring at the blank screen for several minutes, she picked the cell up. She found the phone icon. Opened it. Located the recent calls. At the top of the list she found his number, hit the information symbol, and then tapped the screen to add it to her contacts. In the space provided for a name, she typed in all caps one word—ASSHOLE—hit the save button and picked up her wine glass.

CHAPTER 5

Sunday for Dub moved like molasses in winter. He rose early as always. He knew his friends would all be getting ready for church services, so he did not make the drive into town for coffee, but instead put a pot on at home. While it brewed, he settled into his recliner and opened his Bible. Over the past couple of weeks, he had been studying the gospel of Luke, a chapter a day. Gurgling from the machine indicated the coffee was ready, just as he finished the parable of the prodigal son.

He laid the Bible gently on the arm of the chair and followed the aroma into the kitchen. As he filled his cup, in his mind, he heard his father's voice. *A man's coffee ought to be black and strong enough to float a ten-penny nail.* Once again, the proverb came to mind—"train up a child in the way he should go." It had been many years since he and his father parted ways. Dub, not unlike the prodigal son in the parable, had left home and been lost in the world. He had wondered away from God and the spiritual ways in which he was raised. One of his greatest regrets was that his earthly father had passed on before he found his way back. Dub sipped his coffee and wondered if somehow, wherever his father's spirit was, he knew his son had finally found his way back to the straight and narrow path. Dub found himself hoping his father knew.

The boxes of photographs on the table drew his attention. He ignored them, took his coffee back into the living room, and returned to studying his Bible. An hour later, he had reread the fifteenth chapter of Luke, scanned through several of the

Proverbs, and read Psalms twenty-three twice. *Are you going to keep reading all day just to avoid those pictures, marine?* Once again Sergeant Frye's voice pushed forward.

He knew it was his subconscious reprimanding him for procrastinating, but he found it irritating just the same. His initial reaction to finding the boxes had been to simply toss them out, and as he closed his Bible and laid it aside, he considered it once again. Some memories were better left buried, he told himself. *Spiritual sepsis, gangrene for the soul, go ahead, soldier, just leave those wounds open and exposed.* Sergeant Frye was on a roll this morning. *If you're lucky maybe it'll just leave a big ugly scar on your spirit.*

Empty cup in his hand he rose and returned to the coffee pot. Tired of arguing, he poured it full, sat down at the table, and removed the lid from the first box.

The gong of the grandfather clock sounded ten times as Katherine passed the sitting room on her way to the kitchen for the third time since getting out of bed. She felt sluggish and her head ached. And as far as she was concerned it was all Dub Taylor's fault. The fact that there was an empty wine bottle on the counter beside the refrigerator had nothing to do with it. Everything, including her excessively crappy state of mind, was on Dub.

She filled her coffee cup from the half empty pot, found a bottle of extra-strength pain relievers in the medicine cabinet, and took two. If the day went as usual, Jenn would show up shortly after one. Katherine wondered if a long soak in a hot bubble bath would make her feel better and speculated it would not. *There's no way in hell I'm going to let Jenn find out I woke up hungover,* she thought to herself on her way back to her room.

Setting the coffee on her vanity, she stepped back and looked at herself in the mirror. The simple silk nightgown she wore hung several inches above her knees. It was her favorite color, emerald green, and she liked the way it brought out the color in her eyes. Without support her breasts sagged more than she would have liked but she was proud that they were all natural. She cupped one in each hand and pushed them into what she considered the perfect position.

"What the hell has gotten into you?" she asked the reflection in the mirror as she dropped her hands and let her breasts fall back to their original location. This is why fifty-year-old women don't date, she thought as she picked up the coffee and decided a bath sounded like a good idea after all.

By noon, Dub had made his way through the first box. It was clear that his mother had not bothered to organize the pictures in any particular order. Photos of his parents' wedding were scattered throughout the box, in and amongst black and white photographs of his grandparents and what he assumed was his great-grandparents. None of the pictures had been labeled and so if he did not recognize them, he had no way of knowing who they might have been.

He had carefully placed each photo back in its original place except for seven. A photograph of his mother in a wedding dress. One of her and his father standing together beside their wedding cake. One of each of his grandparents and one he was pretty sure was a picture of his father's grandmother and grandfather standing beside an old tractor. With care, he placed the lid back on the box and set it on the far end of the table.

With no desire to delve into the second box, he decided to fix himself some lunch. He dug a cast-iron skillet out of the drawer below the oven and sat it on the stove top. From the fridge, he gathered a stick of butter, an onion, and the half-pound of ground chuck he had purchased at the grocery store the day before. He dropped a quarter of the stick of butter into the skillet, turned the fire on under it, and while it melted, diced half the onion.

The other half of the onion he sealed in a baggy and placed back in the vegetable drawer. When the butter was completely melted, he cooked the onions until they were transparent, and then added the hamburger meat. A bit of salt and pepper to help season it and while that was browning, he peeled three large potatoes, cut them into small cubes, and rinsed them under the faucet.

The sizzle of the meat cooking combined with the smell of the onions and potatoes, brought a memory of his mother fussing at his older brother, Ben, to stay out of the kitchen and away from the food until she had it on the table. Dub's mind created the day in such vivid detail that he turned to see if his eight-year-old self was standing in the doorway. Ben had laughed, grabbed a freshly made hot roll, and dodged around the other side of the table. She had scolded him playfully then tossed a roll to Dub and told them that better hold them until lunch was ready.

See there's some good memories hidden away in that noggin of yours, Sergeant Frye interrupted the scene. Dub smiled to himself and nodded.

Half an hour later, he turned the fire off under the skillet of hash and waited for the water to boil in the green beans he had dumped from a can into a medium saucepan. While the meat and potatoes had been simmering, he had searched through the kitchen cabinets and drawers in hopes of finding a copy of his mother's bread recipe. He had been unsuccessful.

The bath had helped but not enough. Katherine was not sure if it was the wine from the night before or the thought of getting ready for the coming date that had her brain in a fog. She decided it did not matter.

She was stretched out on her bed in a pair of lightweight, crinkled fabric, lounge pants and an over-sized cotton shirt that had a picture of George Strait and the words "I Hate Everything", when she heard Jenn come through the front door. Instead of getting up and going to meet her daughter, she laid right where she was and listened as Jenn wondered around the house hollering for her.

"What are you doin'?" Jenn asked when she finally stepped through the door and found her.

"Trying to decide what to wear," Katherine decided honesty was the best course of action.

"Wear to what?" Jenn asked, and then in nearly the same instant, did a little dance, and squealed, "You've got a date."

Katherine rolled her head toward her daughter, stared at her in confusion, and said, "I thought you didn't approve of me dating Dub."

"Oh, I don't," Jen's eyes narrowed and her lips pursed for a split second. Then she squealed again, "But you've got a date."

"So you said once already." Katherine rolled her eyes.

Jenn crossed the room to her mother, grabbed her arm, and pulled at her, "Come on get up. We've got to get you ready. How much time do we have?"

Katherine allowed herself to be pulled into a sitting position before pulling away. "We've got plenty of time. He's not picking me up until six."

Jenn stepped back and made a show of studying her mother's outfit. Then she stepped forward and began to fuss with Katherine's hair. Almost instantly, Katherine waved her away and stood up. The loose-fitting t-shirt formed to her body and Jenn's eyes widened.

"Goodness, Momma, you're not wearin' a bra." Jenn placed a hand over her mouth as if shocked.

"Oh, stop it," Katherine shook her head. "I'm not in the mood."

"You are plannin' to wear one tonight, aren't ya?" Jenn grinned and Katherine was not quite sure if she was serious or mocking her.

"I haven't decided yet," she figured two could play that game and felt a slight tinge of pleasure when Jenn's face registered true uncertainty.

Dub cleaned his plate and utensils and the saucepan he had used for green beans and placed them in the dish drainer beside the sink. The skillet he wiped clean and stored back under the stove. He refilled his coffee cup before turning back to the boxes on the table.

I think I've had enough for one day, the thought passed through his mind, and he waited for Sergeant Frye's voice to chastise. It did not come so he pushed his chair in and wandered through the house out the back door onto the porch.

It was time to decide where he was going to take Katherine on their first date. As he stood considering it, he realized that this was actually their second date. It was hard to believe how one horrible event could have such a long-term effect on people's lives. There was no way he could change the past, this he knew. But the future, well, perhaps he could do something to make it a little better for some. He checked his watch. Ten minutes after two, less than four hours until go time. *I reckon I better get to plannin'*, he smiled to himself as he took a sip from the coffee cup.

CHAPTER 6

At six o'clock on the dot, Dub pressed the button for the doorbell beside the front door of Katherine's house. He had been told by Carl that the residence was massive but even with the forewarning, he had been surprised. So much had changed since the last time he had driven onto the William family's property those many years ago. Then the road had been gravel and he had sat proud as a peacock in his old two-tone Chevy truck.

His current truck was an extended cab Silverado and the pavement that led from Katherine's mailbox to her country mansion was well-maintained asphalt that widened into a huge circle drive big enough to park several vehicles. The walkway leading to the front door was aggregated concrete lined with knee-high shrubbery.

The loud ding-dong of the bell sounding inside the house let Dub know the button worked. He stepped back from the door and looked out across the land. Three old oak trees at the base of a ridge a half mile away caught his attention. The terrain looked different but if his memory was accurate, there should have been a house just to the right of those trees. There was not. He knew how cruel time could be but there should be the outline of a foundation. Or at very least an impression where the lane had been.

The sound of footsteps approaching caused him to turn back to the door. Not sure what to expect, he mentally braced himself as the door opened.

"Hello, Mr. Taylor. I'm Jenn, Katherine's daughter," the young woman in front of him spoke fast, took a deep breath as if she had been running, and then with a wave of her hand. "Would you please come in? Momma will be ready in just a couple more minutes."

"Thank you," Dub nodded as he stepped through the door.

The door shut behind him and before he could speak again, Jenn pointed to the room in front of him. "You can have a seat in there." And then she disappeared down a hallway to his left.

Rags to riches, the thought made him smile as he stood and admired the tiled floor and hardwood trim. Katherine had come a long way from the little three-room frame house where she had shared a room with her older sister. He recalled a letter in which his mother had mentioned that one of her grandparents down in Texas had struck oil.

"Must have been one helluva strike." He muttered to himself as he stepped into the sitting room and looked around.

"I don't think I can go through with this." Katherine sat with her head in her hands on the settee with her back to the vanity.

"Oh, yes you can." Jenn stood hands on hips. "You signed up for this and you cannot let him win without even stepping into the ring."

Katherine looked up at her daughter. "This isn't a fight. There are no winners or losers."

"Really?" Jenn maintained her stance. "So what's it all about then? 'Cause we both know you don't need that land."

"You're right," Katherine shook her head in agreement. "I don't need the land. This whole thing was just a crazy stupid mistake. I don't know what I was thinking but now I think we should simply call it off."

"Like hell," Jenn's voice raised. "After all the years of you preaching at me 'bout not takin' shit from no man. Oh, no. I don't know what this is all about, but it reminds me a lot of that time Lacey Tilman threatened to whip my ass. You remember what you told me?"

When Katherine did not respond, Jenn continued, "You said tell her to pick a place and meet her there. So, I did. Remember what happened next?"

"Yeah," Katherine sighed. "She whipped your ass good."

"Yes she did," Jenn punctuated each word she spoke with a finger shake, "but I blooded her nose and knocked out two of her teeth. By the time it was over, we both looked like hell and she never threatened me again."

"And your point is?" Katherine asked.

"My point is," Jenn squinted her eyes, "that you taught me never to run from a fight and I'll be damned if I'll sit by and watch you run from one."

"This is not a fight." Katherine dropped her head back into her hands. "I'm not even sure what it is."

"Well, whatever it is," Jenn stepped up next to her mother, "you ain't gonna run from it."

She softly rubbed her mother's shoulder and waited. Katherine slowly removed her hands from her face and stood up. Turning, she looked at herself in the mirror.

"What is he wearing?" She tugged at the waistband of the light beige pantsuit she had chosen. It was one of her favorites.

"Clothes." Jenn shrugged. A look from Katherine and she elaborated. "A white western shirt, jeans, boots, and he was holding a hat in his hands."

"Maybe I'm overdressed." Katherine ran her hand over the V-neck blouse she wore under her jacket.

"You're not overdressed," Jenn shook her head and exhaled sharply. "You are, however, stalling. Now put your shoes on, it's time to go."

The click of heels on tile warned Dub of Katherine's approach several seconds before she came into his view. The beige pantsuit screamed fancy business meeting and the matching three-inch wedges she had chosen gave her enough lift that the two saw eye-to-eye, if only physically. Jenn stood beside her mother looking frazzled.

"Are we ready, then?" Dub fought the urge to look at his watch, instead motioning towards the door and offering her an arm.

"As we will ever be." Katherine refused the arm and opened the door herself.

Dub followed her out, leaving Jenn standing in the open doorway. At the truck, he stepped quickly around and opened the door for Katherine.

"You have her home by midnight!" Jenn hollered from the entry way with a grin. "And you kids don't do anything I wouldn't do."

Dub failed to suppress a grin. Instead of waiting for him to close the door, Katherine reached out and slammed it shut herself. Still grinning, Dub turned and shrugged at Jenn, who shrugged back with a smirk of her own before retreating into the house.

A quick trip around to his side of the vehicle and Dub opened the driver's side door to find Katherine already seat belted in staring straight ahead with her chin slightly raised. He waited until he had started the engine and the pickup was rolling before he spoke.

"Well, Kat, how was your day?" he asked as he eased around what he figured was Jenn's car and navigated the circle.

He was beginning to think she was not going to respond, when without even a sideways glance in his direction, in a tone just slightly warmer than an artic iceberg she said, "Very enlightening, if I do say so. This afternoon, I was contemplating Darwin, and his idea that we might have evolved from lower life forms, and while I have always considered the notion preposterous, I do believe it may have some merit seeing how it's becoming clearer to me with the passing of every second that you most likely descended from a jackass."

Dub raised one hand off the steering wheel and waved it over his head. "Amen to that sister," he laughed heartily.

37

When Dub slowed to a stop at the end of her driveway, Katherine considered opening the truck door and jumping out. She knew it was a stupid idea. The odds of her landing upright in high heels was astronomical. And if she did manage to survive it, there was the long walk back to the house because she sure as hell was not calling Jenn for a ride.

Dub turned right onto the county road and pointed the truck towards town. Katherine wondered where he was taking her but refused to ask.

By the time he turned on Main Street she felt like she was going to burst if she did not say something. The only sounds since they had passed her mailbox were the hum of the truck wheels on the road and the occasional tap of Dub's thumb on the steering wheel which for some reason annoyed her more with each dull thump.

As they passed the Sonic, she reached over and turned the radio on expecting to hear a radio station, instead she heard a click and the whine of a compact disc starting up. The sound of the fiddle intro to *Fool Hearted Memory* filled the cab followed by George Strait's voice.

Her first thought was to turn it off quickly. She wondered if he had set it up like that on purpose and if so, she would not let it get to her. As the lyrics mentioned an old love that could not be forgotten, she set her jaw and stared at the road ahead.

The second verse started, and Dub added his voice to the song. It was all that Katherine could do not to scream. He slowed to let a line of cars pass then turned into a parking spot in front of Dairy Queen, turned the key in the ignition, and continued to sing until the lyrics ended. As the final note faded, he opened the door and the stereo shut itself off.

Dairy Queen, you have got to be kidding me! Katherine could feel the heat of her anger rush from the collar of her blouse upward and hoped it would not melt her makeup. She was not going to let him get to her. If this was what the land cost then so be it, but Dairy Queen, hell she could have worn her jogging outfit. Jenn's voice broke through, *yeah, right, mom, like you'd be caught dead in town in the clothes you run in.*

Dub opened the door and offered a hand to help her down. *If this is the game you want to play,* she thought as she took it. As soon as she had her feet firmly on the ground, she released his hand and walked beside him to the door. She waited and allowed him to open it for her before stepping into the building.

Instantly the aroma of hamburgers and fries hit her like a wave of nostalgia. The sound of a milkshake machine's metallic whirl and the sizzle of grease from the kitchen fueled a dozen memories. None of which she was ready to face. Without waiting on Dub, she turned and made her way to the back of the room, ignoring the stares of the other patrons. Well aware of how overdressed she was and her subconscious urge to run, she slid into a corner booth with her back to the counter.

Dub eased onto the bench across the table from her and smiled. It took all the willpower she could muster not to reach across and slap the grin from his face.

"When was the last time you were in here?" he continued to smile.

She glared at him and even though she told her brain not to go there, it seemed to have a mind of its own. A long-forgotten memory from high school surfaced. Rough and cloudy along the edges she refused to let it take form. "Sometime when I was in high school."

"That long, huh?" he raised his eyebrows. "And after all this time, you still came right to our booth."

Beneath the table top she squeezed the edge of her seat with both hands and cursed herself mentally for not remembering. At every turn something was reminding her of the past and she did not like it.

"I don't think much has changed," Dub nodded past her head at the menu above the counter, "would you like a hamburger, or do you still only eat fries and a chocolate shake on a date?"

"I'm not hungry," the tone of her voice caused several heads to turn.

Dub's eyes met hers, "Fries and a shake it is then," and before she could respond he slid from the booth and was headed for the counter.

CHAPTER 7

It bothered Dub very little that all eyes were on him as he left the counter and returned to his seat across from Katherine carrying a receipt which included the number of his order. He had not expected the evening to go well and so far Katherine had not disappointed.

"Why are you doing this?" she hissed just above a whisper as soon as he was seated.

It would have been better had she just spoken in her normal voice. The sound of her anger, no matter how softly spoken, caught the attention of most of the people in the room. Those more polite folks managed to control the urge to turn and look. Others were not as understanding, and one young man even reached for his cellphone before Dub shot him a look that said it was not a good idea.

"You wanted my land," he shrugged.

"Yes, but I could have paid you for it." Katherine's voice had not lost its edge, "Why this?"

"I did not need nor want your money," Dub rubbed a finger along the side of his chin and considered how much he should tell her. "Money would only have complicated my future plans."

He watched Katherine's expression as she tried to digest this new bit of information. To someone who had built her whole being around her wealth, it must seem odd to her that he did not want her money. The young man who had reached for his phone rose quickly from the booth where he had been seated and joined by his two companions made his way out the front door.

"What future plans?" Katherine's question was exactly what he had expected.

"That's not part of the deal." He smiled as a burly young man with a big baritone voice called his number from the front. "Be right back."

He paused briefly on his way to the register as a young family of four eased out of their booth and left, then continued on to the counter. He picked up the tray with his order and balanced it in one hand, stepped to the self-help counter and gathered napkins and individually wrapped plastic utensils before snaking his way in between booths on his way back to Katherine. As he sat the tray on the table in front of her, the last two sets of customers left through the side door leaving the building empty except for the fellow working the cash register and drive-thru window and a cook.

Dub took the burger basket he had ordered and placed it on his side of the table before sliding into his seat. Reaching over, he took his glass of sweet tea leaving only Katherine's fries and milkshake on the tray in front of her.

"If you're trying to remind me of the way it used to be," she said with a wave of her hands across the ice cream in front of her, "it won't work."

"Maybe it will, maybe it won't." Dub smiled and arranged the burger so that he could eat it with one hand and use his other for his drink and fries.

"You will never win my heart again." Katherine's eyes were little more than slits.

With a nod of agreement, Dub leaned slightly forward before speaking. "That was never my intent. I lost the right to your heart a long time ago. And just so you know, it is very near, if not at the top, of my list of regrets. But winning it back is not why I asked for our little arrangement."

When he finished speaking, he took a bite from the burger and began to chew. As he watched, Katherine picked up a fry and dipped it into her shake. As she raised it towards her mouth, Dub thought, *one step at a time, maybe there's hope after all.*

Katherine stared down at her last fry. She had forgotten how good the salt mixed with the chocolate tasted when she dipped them in her shake. She stirred the last of the ice cream with her straw before popping the last fry into her mouth, then she sucked the last of the now melted liquid from the bottom of her cup. The noise made by the lack of suction as air filled the straw made her smile. It had been years since she had done that and while it might not be considered ladylike, tonight she just did not give a damn.

Dub had finished his meal and was sipping on his tea when she sat the empty cup down on the tray. *Date one down*, she thought, *all that's left is the ride home.*

Gathering his trash, Dub placed it on the tray with hers, and rose to leave. She followed his lead. A brief stop at the trash can to dump the tray and he opened the door for her. The sun had disappeared sometime during their meal leaving the parking lot bathed in artificial light. Dub followed her to the passenger side of the truck, opened the door, and stood there while she climbed up into her seat. She allowed him to shut the door himself and watched as he made his way around the vehicle.

She found it hard to imagine the next six dates would all be visits to the Dairy Queen but if they were she decided she was okay with it. Of course, her choice of clothing would be adjusted accordingly.

Dub opened his door, settled himself behind the wheel, and turned the key in the ignition. The compact disc whirled and the piano intro to George Strait's *Marina del Rey* began. Dub reached over, tapped a button, and the song changed to *Amarillo By Morning*. As he backed out into the street, George began to sing.

Main Street faded behind them and it was not until he passed the turn for her house that Katherine realized there was more to the date than just a trip to Dairy Queen. She looked over her shoulder to make sure she was not mistaken and then said to Dub, "You missed the turn."

"Got one more stop to make," he stared straight ahead, and Katherine got the feeling that he was staring down some demon out there in the dark past the lights of the truck.

The road curved east and then straightened out. Just before they reached the Nida Baptist Church, he slowed and took a sharp turn onto the road Katherine knew led to Milburn. With care he pulled off the shoulder and onto the grass. Several minutes passed while Dub sat staring out the window.

"As far as I can figure, this is the spot," Dub broke the silence. "Right here is where my life changed. And because of that, in more ways than I care to admit, your life changed. Right here. One carefree second. One stupid kid. One horrific accident."

The last three words escaped as more of a choke than actual words. That Dub was having trouble holding his feelings in was not lost on Katherine.

"It was not your fault." She heard herself whisper.

Dub opened the door and stepped out. The dome light illuminated the road to the centerline. Katherine watched as he looked back around the curve that led to Nida. He turned back and looked deep into her eyes. "I know that now but back then I thought it was and it all but killed me."

A part of her wanted to hold him, to forget the past, and simply wrap her arms around him. A memory stronger and more ferocious pushed past it and she said, "It was not my fault either." And the tears started to flow.

"I never thought it was your fault," Dub said as he climbed back into the truck, "never."

"Then why didn't you tell me that? Why didn't you say something to me? Anything to me?" Katherine asked as she wiped at the tears with the back of her hand. "I thought you hated me because you thought it was my fault and it was more than I could take. Why? Why did you...?"

Dub opened the center console and handed Katherine a stack of napkins. "Because I was stupid. Because I was just a kid. Because I was mad at the world, and I didn't know how to deal with it."

"You broke my heart." Katherine managed to whisper through the sniffles.

"And I am sorry for that," Dub used a napkin to wipe the moisture from beneath his own eyes. "I'm sorry for a lot of things. And if I'm bein' honest, most of my regrets, most of the things I'm sorry for, most of the negativity in my life originated right here in this very spot."

Katherine managed to get the tears under control and thought about what he had said, "So, what. Is this some kind of twelve-step program where you hope to make things all better for yourself?"

"Not at all," he said and eased the truck back onto the road. "This isn't about me."

Katherine shook her head, "Then who is it about?"

At the intersection, he made the turn that would take them back towards Tishomingo and home. "It's about you."

Confused and angry, she stared at him. He kept his eyes on the road in front of the vehicle until finally, she said, "I'm just fine."

With a quick glance her way, in a tone soft and low, he said, "But are you really?"

She was still trying to configure a response when he left her at the door to her house and walked back out to his truck.

CHAPTER 8

Monday morning found Dub seated in his recliner, Bible across his lap and a cup of coffee on the end table beside him. He had contemplated a trip into town but the idea of being grilled by Carl had changed his mind. It was not so much the thought of discussing the date that kept him home. Since he had told no one his plans, there would be few that knew the date had even happened. Of course, by the end of the day, the local gossip tree would change that, he was sure. After some careful self-examination, he knew his own mental and emotional state was questionable, and the thought of Carl poking and prying was not appealing.

He picked up the coffee cup, took a sip, and set it back in its place. The Bible verse he had just read wiggled its way through the recesses of his mind. Opening a door here. Pulling at the edge of a memory there. He looked down and scanned the verse once again. "For a just man falleth seven times, and riseth up again: but the wicked shall fall into mischief."

Seven times. He wondered how many times he had fallen. More than seven times, he was sure, more likely the seven times seventy Jesus spoke of in Matthew if he remembered his Bible correctly. The notion that even the tiniest bit of his spirit had survived so many falls still amazed him. It was not that he thought of himself as righteous by any means. It was simply that after so many years and so much time spent wallowing in the world's cesspool of sin and his own self-destructiveness, he found it hard to understand how any good was left in him. And yet, here he was doing his best to follow the path God had set before him.

"The prayers of a righteous man availeth much," came to his mind. He picked up his phone and after a quick search found the verse came from the fifth chapter of James. He smiled, knowing that it was not only the prayers of men that had protected what he figured was the last smidgin of his soul. In his mind, the prayers of his mother were the ones that had made the biggest difference.

He had seen the underbelly of civilization. He had walked through the valley of death. The Gulf War, his introduction to the darkness, had been one of the first of many spiritual falls. Multiple tours in Afghanistan had increased the number, but it was not only his military career that had soured him. Two failed marriages and a string of bad relationships had taken plenty out of him as well.

He closed the Bible, laid his phone on the end table, picked up his coffee cup, and made his way into the kitchen. He topped off his cup, shut off the machine, and leaned back against the counter. The boxes on the table needed his attention and since he could think of no reason not to, he decided the box labeled—60 TO 64—would be his project for the morning.

At one-thirty Monday afternoon, Jenn found her mother sitting at the kitchen bar holding a large empty mug. Katherine's silk nightgown could be seen through the gap in the terrycloth robe she had loosely tied around her waist. Her feet were bare, her hair was piled atop her head in what some would call a messy bun and she had not bothered to apply her makeup. Jenn could not recall a time in her life when her mother had left the bedroom before dressing, fixing her hair, and making sure her face looked presentable.

Jenn was not sure whether it was some kind of breakthrough or a seriously overdue breakdown. "Are you okay, mom?" The confusion in her voice was audible.

Katherine looked up at her and in the softest tone Jenn had

ever heard come from her mother said, "I've been trying to figure that out all morning."

Unsure what to do, Jenn eased the mug from her mother's hands. She looked inside and realized it had held coffee at some point. "Would you like a refill?" she asked.

"Yeah, that sounds good," Katherine responded and nodded over her shoulder towards the machine on the counter.

The pot was still half full, so she took a second cup from the cabinet, and made herself a mug after filling Katherine's. She handed her mother's coffee to her and then pulled one of the tall bar chairs around so she could sit next to her. The two sat quietly until Jenn leaned over and whispered, "You want to talk about it?"

"Maybe." Katherine ran a finger along the handle of the mug but did not look up.

"Okay." Jenn blew softly across the top of her mug.

Jenn had taken several sips of her coffee before Katherine spoke again. "Is there something wrong with me?" she looked into her daughter's eyes as she spoke.

Jenn sat her coffee aside and gathered her mother's hands in her own. "Mom it's after two o'clock in the afternoon. You're still in your nightgown and you haven't done your hair. Yes, I'd say there is something wrong with you."

Katherine looked down at the robe she was wearing and then back up at Jenn, "Not just today. Everyday, all the time, is there something wrong with me?"

"I don't know." Jenn felt at a loss. "I reckon there's probably something wrong with all of us on one level or another."

Katherine nodded and looked away. Jenn studied her mother's face as Katherine stared across the kitchen lost in thought. The ice machine dumped in the refrigerator and the soft buzz of the water refilling the tray added the soundtrack to a scene stranger than Jenn could ever have imagined. If she had not just spent a full morning cutting hair at the salon, she might have been able to convince herself she was still asleep.

"Two o'clock?" A hint of confusion strained Katherine's voice. "Why aren't you at work?"

"My last appointment was at noon," Jenn explained, then asked, "What happened last night?"

Katherine looked at her, but Jenn got the feeling that she was not so much looking at her as she was looking through her. It was eerie and she found herself worried that something had pushed her mother over the edge. If Dub Taylor had done her mother harm, she would shoot him, by all that she found holy, she would.

"What happened with Mr. Taylor last night, Mom?" Jenn clapped her hands together in hopes it might bring Katherine out of whatever state she was in.

"I think he tried to make amends," Katherine smiled. "He said he was sorry, and I believed him. But then he said it was about me and when I told him I was fine, do you know what he said?"

When Jenn realized Katherine was waiting on an answer, she shook her head and said, "No, Mom, I don't know what he said."

"He said, but are you really?" Katherine looked into Jenn's eyes. "Like maybe he knew something I didn't. And ever since then, I've been searching for the answer."

"Good Lord, Momma," Jenn felt like she had been holding her breath for half an hour. "You've got to snap out of it. He's just a man. You haven't seen him in how many years? He's only been back in town, what? Maybe six months? He doesn't know you and he sure doesn't know anything about you that you don't know about yourself."

Katherine smiled. "You weren't there, Jenn. You didn't hear the way he said it. And he took me to the spot where it happened."

Jenn stared at her mother and waited, but Katherine just sat there and smiled. Jenn was not sure if a good old-fashioned slap would bring her out of whatever this was or not, but she was very close to giving it a try. Finally unable to handle the pressure any longer, the volume of her voice slightly raised and a bit forceful, she said, "The spot where what happened?"

49

The smile faded from Katherine's face, "Oh, my, you don't know about the accident."

Jenn threw up her hands, "What accident, Mom?"

Katherine reached over and patted her on the knee. "I forget that we lived in Ardmore during your growing up years, so of course you wouldn't know. And it was so long ago, nobody talks about it anymore."

"Mom, you're talking in circles." Jenn snapped her fingers twice. "Can we focus on the accident?"

"It's funny how no matter how tragic an event is," Katherine continued, "as time passes, it just seems to fade away. After a few years, people move on, and a few more years go by, and…"

"Mom, please," Jenn pleaded.

Katherine pushed her coffee mug away and laid her hands on the countertop. Jenn watched as her mother flexed the fingers on each hand then gently placed them on the marble surface.

"I was a sophomore in high school when it happened," Katherine stared at the back of her hands as she spoke softly. "It was homecoming week. Football homecoming. The boys won the game and afterwards there was a big party."

Katherine paused and rubbed her thumb across the nail of her index finger. Jenn could hear the lup-dup of each beat of her own heart as she waited.

"I went with Dub. Your Aunt Vickie went with Ben, Dub's older brother. It was out in the middle of someone's pasture. I can't remember whose. I wonder why I can't remember. Seems like I would remember that, but I don't." Katherine moved her middle finger in a circular pattern just above the bridge of her nose as if the motion would bring a name forward.

"And?" Jenn leaned forward and prompted.

"There was a lot of drinking going on. Mostly beer, but a couple of the guys brought some bottles of… I can't remember exactly… whiskey, I think." Katherine sighed, looked up briefly, and then back at her hands. "Dub and I were sitting on the tailgate of Ben's pickup. We weren't drinking. Dub didn't like the taste of beer and I was afraid your grandparents would find out if I did, but Ben was really celebrating."

"The accident?" Jenn redirected.

"Vickie got mad at Ben and wanted to go home." Katherine knit her brows together and glared at hands, "Dub and I were enjoying the evening and weren't ready to leave. Tim Jackson's girlfriend, I don't remember her name. She didn't go to school with us. I can't remember what school she went to, maybe Caddo."

Jenn could feel the tension as Katherine gritted her teeth and balled her hands into fists. Slowly Katherine turned to face her daughter. "It was the first time he ever kissed me. It was not supposed to end. It was supposed to be the beginning of something beautiful and then… and then the accident happened, and Ben died."

For a second, Jenn thought her heart might stop. Her breath caught and it was a second before she managed to get out, "How? What happened?"

As if she realized she had skipped too far ahead, Katherine shook her head. Jenn could almost see her mother's mind reversing course. "Dub told Ben to go. He told him to come back and get us later. So, Ben and Vickie, and Tim and his girlfriend, all loaded up in Ben's truck and left. Vickie told me later Tim's girlfriend had to go home, too, and that's where the other three were headed after they dropped Vickie off."

Katherine stopped and began to draw imaginary lines on the countertop. First towards herself and then her finger took a hard right tracing a straight line that ended in front of Jenn. A quick tap and it reversed course and ran back past Katherine to the far edge of the counter, made a big circle and started back. "At Nida, just this side of the Baptist Church, where highways twenty-two and seventy-eight intersect," she tapped hard with her finger, "Ben pulled around this curve. I heard someone say once that Tim said they both needed to pee. I think they'd had a few more beers. I guess Ben thought he had pulled off the highway. I don't think he ever knew the truck hit him."

"Oh, my," Jenn released the breath she had not realized she was holding. "That is awful. Oh, Mom, that had to be hard."

"After that night, the Dub I knew just kind of disappeared." Katherine's voice broke as Jenn watched a tear escape from her eye, trace a path down her cheek, and drop on the counter. Jenn eased out of her seat and wrapped her arms around her mother. As her own tears began to flow, she wondered how long the pain of that night had been locked away deep inside this woman that she loved.

CHAPTER 9

"I am beginning to feel like a kindergarten teacher at recess," Mason Boyd interrupted the argument between Dub and Katherine.

In the silence that followed, Katherine turned her glare from Dub to Mason. The red in her face warned him that, if not careful, he would indeed be receiving his very own personal cussing session.

"I got your last statement." Mason turned at Dub's voice, "and I'm pretty sure you get paid a lot more than a kindergarten teacher. And in my opinion that in itself is a crime."

The grin on Dub's face let him know that his client was thoroughly enjoying this morning's meeting. With a pleading look that was meant to suggest a bit more understanding on Dub's part, but in reality, came across as desperation, he turned his attention back to Katherine, "Mrs. Williams, if I am hearing what you are saying correctly, you would like for Mr. Taylor to give you the days and times he plans to take you out on the agreed dates."

"Yes, that is correct," Katherine nodded. "Six days and times, so I can put the appointments into my calendar, plus the places where he plans for us to go."

Mason looked to Dub, who smiled, "No can do."

"Why is that?" Mason asked as he noticed the fire in Katherine's eyes.

"Because," Dub gave a shrug, "I don't know the days or times, or even where we are going to go. I guess you could say, I'm just makin' it up as I go."

"Making it up as you go!! Making it up as you go!!" Katherine turned to Dub and for the next several minutes, Mason felt like he was watching a verbal tennis match. Katherine would shout and cuss until she finally arrived at a question. Dub sat calmly waiting for said question to arrive on his side of the net, then with the ease of a professional he would grin and send the ball soaring back.

When it became apparent that the two of them could and would continue the rally all day, Mason slammed his hand down on his desk. "Okay, you two, this is getting us nowhere."

He made sure he had both of their attention before proceeding. "Mr. Taylor would it be possible for you to at least have a plan from one date to the next. Let's say for instance, that you give it a few minutes of thought and decide here today when date number two will take place."

Katherine gave Dub a side-eyed glance before turning her glare back on the attorney. Dub rubbed his chin, "Next Monday at three o'clock."

That's odd, Mason thought, but hopeful of peaceful dialogue turned to Katherine, "Does that work for you?"

"And where would we be going?" Katherine snarled once again, only half turning to look at Dub.

"Let's call it an early dinner," Dub grinned, "and I haven't decided on the exact place, so I guess that part will have to be a surprise."

"Like the Dairy Queen surprise?" The volume of Katherine's voice was beginning to rise again. "Or the trip out to Nida?"

Dub held his hands up. *As if that will shield you from her wrath*, Mason thought, but wisely did not verbalize.

"No Dairy Queen. No Nida." Dub moved one hand to cover his heart. "I promise. Nothing like that again. Just a nice dinner. You, me, and a little conversation."

Katherine continued to glare at him. Mason watched as her features softened slightly. She turned away from Dub and adjusted the front of her jacket, "What should I wear?"

From Dub's expression, Mason could tell he was about to say something smart. He gave him a sharp look and Dub shrugged, "Whatever you would normally wear on a nice dinner date."

Mason waited and when neither Katherine nor Dub seemed to have anything more to add, he summarized, "So, date number two will be Monday at three o'clock. This being Wednesday, that is five days from today. The date will be a dinner date. And I suggest we plan to meet back here on the Wednesday after so the two of you can agree on plans for date number three. Are we in agreement?"

A nod of understanding was all he got from either of them. Figuring he would take what he could get, he stood. When neither of them took the hint that the meeting had concluded, he raised an eyebrow. "Are there any further questions?"

With a shake of his head, Dub stood and started for the door. Katherine followed and paused several feet behind him when he stopped to retrieve his Stetson from the rack. As the door shut behind the two, Mason pulled open his desk drawer and reached for the key to the file cabinet.

Sunday morning found Dub seated in the next to the last pew at the First Baptist Church on Main Street in Tishomingo. It was his third visit. Carl had invited him each time and while he enjoyed the message, he found the acoustics more to his liking at the First United Methodist Church. Carl and his wife, Ida, had invited him to sit with them in their pew closer to the front but he had declined. Years of military training and the need to assess the whole situation made it easier on his mind to find a seat behind the congregation with a view of all entry points.

The preacher at the altar was speaking about cleaning the inside of the cup and platter so that the inside would also be clean. When someone off to his left shouted amen, Dub realized he had tuned out somewhere along the way.

"You can put on pretty clothes. You can drive a nice car and look every part the Christian, but folks, the Good Lord can see the inside of the cup." The preacher paused there for effect, letting the words settle on the congregation.

Dub tried to recall what book of the Bible the man had said he taken his sermon from, but was unable to do so. He made a mental note to look into it when the service was over. The preacher continued and Dub's thoughts turned to Katherine and their upcoming date. When the congregation was dismissed half an hour later, he could not have told you anything about the message except for cleaning the inside of the cup and platter, but he had completely planned out date number two.

"I have appointments all afternoon tomorrow," Jenn was curled up in the corner of the sectional that wrapped around two sides of the den, "so I won't be here when Mr. Taylor picks you up at three."

Katherine did a one shoulder shrug and picked up a piece of the puzzle she was putting together on the coffee table. "I'm sure I'll be fine. I think I can dress myself for a dinner date. I am a grown ass woman, you know?"

Jenn shook her head and chuckled. "This from the same grown ass woman that nearly had a breakdown before her date last week and another the day after the date."

"I'll be fine," Katherine rolled her eyes and shook her head as she spoke then worked the puzzle piece into its spot before picking up another.

Jenn watched as she tried unsuccessfully to place the new piece in several different places before giving up and exchanging it. She had always found her mother's fascination with puzzles odd. No one else in the family much cared for them, but that had never deterred Katherine. What was even more interesting was that after finishing one, she would make sure each piece had been completely separated from the whole and from any other piece before putting them all back in the box. After which she donated them or passed them on. Jenn had no idea to whom. All she was sure of was that she had never seen her mother put the same puzzle together twice.

"Mom, the story you told me about Mr. Taylor's brother the other day kind of left me with some questions." Jenn tilted her head. "Think it would be okay if I asked a couple of them?"

Katherine eased herself from her spot on the floor onto the sectional. She gave the puzzle piece in her hand a gentle toss back onto the table. "I think so."

"You said the Dub you knew disappeared," Jenn watched her mother's face closely. "What did you mean by that?"

Katherine drew her eyebrows down and picked at a piece of lint on the side of her pants. "Dub never was very outgoing. From the time we were kids, he was always kind of quiet and kept to himself, but as we got older, I guess you could say we understood each other," she paused, and Jenn realized she was trying to find the right words to explain what was in her mind. "Maybe it was our similar family dynamics. I don't know. I had one older sister and then there was me. Dub had one older brother and himself. Two families each with two kids. Your Aunt Vicky and Dub's brother Ben... well, it was kind of like they were two people cut from the same cloth. I think that's why they fought as much as they did. Vicky was captain of the cheer team. Ben was the starting quarterback. They were the golden kids. Me and Dub... sometimes, I guess it was like we were just there. Like living in their shadows."

"That doesn't sound like much fun." Jenn leaned forward.

"I didn't mind really," Katherine smiled. "I think that's what caused me and Dub to grow so close. At first it was just two friends who could talk about similar feelings. But then somewhere along the way... well, it was probably me that felt it first. Dub didn't come around until a couple years later, or at least if it was earlier, he was too shy or too awkward to show it. But the summer between my freshman and sophomore year, we started to share more… not just our feelings about how others treated us, but also how we felt about each other. It seemed crazy at first. We were both afraid it would ruin our friendship, so we were… goodness, how clichéd does that sound, but back then… oh, I don't know. Anyway, it all kind of led up to him asking me to be his date for homecoming. He even bought me a corsage. Then after the accident, he wouldn't talk to me at all. Wouldn't talk to anyone."

Jenn waited until she was sure her mother wasn't going to continue, then said, "So, he didn't actually disappear, he just didn't want to talk to anyone?"

"No." Katherine shook her head, looked into her daughter's eyes, and gave a weak smile, "it was more than not just talking to anyone. Dub never returned to school. I went over to his house a couple of times, but his mother told me he did not want to see anyone. She was very kind about it and I could tell she was hurting herself, so I quit going. I guess I thought eventually he would get past it and when he was ready, he would come around again. He missed the whole rest of the year and the next year when school started, he didn't show up. It wasn't long after that I heard he had enlisted in the Marines and left home."

"I see," Jenn said, "he disappeared, just like you said."

"For over forty years." Katherine nodded. "I was heart broke. Then I was furious. Then I forgot about him, or at least I told myself I did, until his mother died, and I heard he was back. Then out of nowhere, I got mad all over."

"Are you sure you don't need me here tomorrow?" Jenn reached across the space between them and took her mother's hand, "I can reschedule my appointments or see if Lori can work them in to her schedule."

"Thanks, but I'll be okay," Katherine smiled. "I think it's about time this grown ass woman learned to put her big girl panties on by herself."

"Alright," Jenn patted her hand. "But I'm just a phone call away if you have any problems."

CHAPTER 10

Katherine did not wait for Dub to ring the bell but stepped out the door and pulled it shut as soon as she saw him stop in the drive. The way he had to scramble out of the truck and hustle around the vehicle to get to the passenger door before she did brought joy to her heart. *One point for me,* she thought, then chastised herself mentally for keeping score. *My goodness, what has gotten into me? If I had not worn these heels, he would have never made it in time.*

"Good afternoon, Kat." Dub said as she stepped up into her seat. *One point to you,* she could not help herself, *but the date is young.* She pulled the hem of her dress away from the edge of the door and nodded at him to let him know she was ready.

Dub gently pushed the door closed and she watched as he made his way back around to his side and even managed a smile when he pulled himself up behind the steering wheel. He had left the vehicle running and she noticed the stereo was not playing. She found herself wondering if it was a setup and decided if there was to be music, he would have to do the honors.

At the end of her driveway, he turned right onto the road and the thought that it was going to be another long silent boring ride had just entered her mind when Dub asked, "What's your opinion on fried chicken?"

At the sound of his voice, she glanced his way. The question caused her to do a double take to see if he was serious. Her reaction brought a smile to his face and a quick look her way.

"Fried chicken?" Katherine repeated the words while she formed a response, "I don't eat a lot of fried food anymore, but

Momma used to make some of the best fried chicken you would ever want to eat. Why do you ask?"

"Just wonderin'," he said as the smile on his face widened. "Do you still drink sweet tea?"

"On occasion," she cut her eyes around at him. "Where is this coming from?"

"You'll see." He winked at her as he pulled to a stop at the intersection of the country road and the state highway. He looked both ways and then turned left.

That they were heading towards Tishomingo was clear. With Durant behind them, Katherine wondered if the date was going to take them to Ardmore or perhaps even to Ada. She found herself hoping that he was not planning on driving all the way to the Oklahoma City area. She was not sure she wanted to spend that much time in the confines of the vehicle with him.

"How far are we going?" she queried, not really expecting a solid answer but figuring it could not hurt to ask.

"Not far," he slowed as the edge of the city limits came into view. "Just a little spot I think you'll enjoy."

She gave him a look she meant as a warning against any foolery. He chuckled and stopped at the redlight at the intersection of Byrd Street and Main. His eyes on the light, he said, "It's not Dairy Queen, I promise."

"It better not be any other fast food place, either." She warned as the light changed and he accelerated.

"It ain't," he raised a hand off the steering wheel to signify his honesty, but the sparkle in his eyes was not the reassurance Katherine was needing.

When he turned north on Kemp, she decided Ada must be their destination and tried to recall which of the restaurants in town she had heard good things about. After just three blocks he slowed and turned onto West Seventh street, and she forgot all about Ada and its eateries.

"Where in the hell are you taking me?" She asked, not sure she really wanted to know the answer.

"On a dinner date." Dub attempted a serious look, but Katherine could see the laughter in his eyes.

Before she could form another question, Dub made a left turn, and she knew exactly where they were going. There was only one destination at the end of the street they were on and it was not the five star establishment she had envisioned, as a matter of fact, it was not an establishment at all. It was the parking area above the old Pennington Creek dam.

The creek started north of Tishomingo and flowed south to Lake Texoma. It cut through the little college town and at some point, well before Katherine's memories began, it had been dammed. Like most of the kids she had grown up with, it was a spot she had frequented often, especially during the hot summer months of her youth. The parking area above the dam was unpaved. On occasion the city would haul in a load of granite gravel. Because no one had ever bothered to level the area, any significant rainfall that followed would wash out large areas of the lot's surface.

Once parked, visitors would work their way across the uneven ground to a trail that led to a set of old concrete stairs. The stairs were steep and narrow, and the only safe means of getting to the area below the dam unless you were young and stupid enough to dive off the old well house, which was at least twenty feet above the top of the dam.

"You have got to be shitting me." She exclaimed as he pulled to a stop on the uneven parking area. The hood of the truck was a good five feet lower in elevation than the tailgate and Katherine was pretty sure if she tried to open her door and step out, the weight of it would send her flying through the air.

"Not at all," the grin had returned to Dub's face, "A nice picnic dinner beside the creek, what could be better than that?"

"Dub Taylor, you had better be kidding me." Katherine warned, "You know there's at least fifty of those concrete steps that lead down to the gravel bar and I'm in heels. Even if I liked the idea, which I do not, do you remember how narrow those damn steps are?"

"I reckon you'll be just fine," Dub eased his door open as he spoke. "Just carry your shoes down in one hand and use the other to hold on to the rail."

"The rail... the rail, good Lord, Dub it was all bent to hell forty years ago when we were kids. I'm not even sure if it's still there," Katherine threw her hands up, "and I'm wearing pantyhose in case you didn't notice."

"Oh, I noticed," Dub said and wiggled his eyebrows. "Kinda thought it was an odd choice of attire for the occasion. You might wanna slip out of them while I get the food and drinks out of the back."

"You, worthless little, son of a bitch!" She shook a fist at him as he shut the door.

She watched as he made his way to the back of the truck and dropped the tailgate. Reaching up under the covered bed he tugged a Yeti cooler out and then noticing that she was watching him, he held up a finger to indicate he would be right back. Carrying the cooler, he disappeared down the path that led to the stairs.

"I will not let him win, I will not," she muttered under her breath as she kicked her heels off and pulled the long skirt up under her bottom. With a quick look around to make sure no one was watching, she wiggled out of the pantyhose. She had barely managed to get herself back together before Dub came strolling up the trail heading back to the truck.

She waited and watched as he gathered a large wicker basket from the back and then shut the tailgate. He carried it to her door then sat it down and with care eased her door open. She took one look at the gravel and knew her feet were too tender to walk on it. With a sigh, she slipped her feet back into the heels and threw her legs around. Even using the running boards on the vehicle, the distance to the ground looked foreboding.

"You have got to be kidding," she looked at Dub with an eyebrow raised and her hand out.

Dub reached up and took it, "My lady."

"You wish," Katherine started down and lost her footing.

"Gotcha," Dub said as she fell into his arms. She had no choice but to wrap hers around him. When she finally regained her balance, all that was needed to complete the picture of the perfect couple was the kiss. One of her feet was even off the ground as if in some crazy way fate was attempting to rule the day.

"You are such a jackass!" Katherine dropped the foot and steadied herself.

"Can't say that I disagree, my lady." Dub chuckled, retrieved the food basket, and without a look back started down the trail once again.

Careful not to catch a heel in one of the many cracks and crevices created by rain runoff, she picked her away along until she reached the top of the stairs leading down. The sound of water cascading over the old dam reminded her of high school days and summers spent stretched out on the gravel bar with friends… with Dub. It only added fuel to her frustration as she grabbed the worn bent single rail and used it to steady herself while she removed her shoes.

The heels in one hand and a tight grip on the rail with her other, she started down muttering obscenities under her breath as she went. The steps were even narrower than she had remembered, and halfway down the thought that she would have to climb back up them later hit. She paused and looked back over her shoulder. For a second, she stood there considering whether or not she should continue her descent or just say the hell with it and turn around. Pride won the battle.

The humidity and heat of the day mixed with her own exertion had caused her to perspire. As she stepped off of the concrete and onto the gravel, the beads that had been gathering gave way to gravity. *I'm sweating*, she thought as she worked her way across the rough stones to where Dub was spreading an enormous blanket. *I hate to sweat. I absolutely hate it.*

Dub looked up with a grin. "You made it. I knew you could."

"I don't like you very much right now," Katherine spoke through gritted teeth and dropped her shoes on the edge of the blanket.

"Humph," Dub chuckled. "That's an improvement."

Beyond caring about manners, Katherine plopped down beside her shoes and glared up at him. "How do you figure?"

"A week and a half ago you didn't like me at all." He winked, opened the cooler, and offered her a bottle of sweet tea.

She made a very un-lady-like noise that sounded something like a horse blowing and flipped him the bird before taking the container from his hand. Her gesture brought on a bout of laughter from Dub that at first made her roll her eyes, "Think you're pretty damn funny don't you?"

"No, I think you're funny," he managed between chuckles. "What a sound," and he did a very poor imitation of it, "And then the bird. My gosh, Kat, it's like were back in high school again."

"Really?" she was finding it hard to stay mad. "When did I ever flip you the bird in high school?"

Dub opened the food basket before he answered, "You never did. Actually, I don't think you would have ever done that back then. I guess I just bring out the…"

"Go to hell, Dub Taylor," Katherine interrupted. "You don't bring out anything in me."

"Alright. Alright." He handed her a plate. "Truce?"

She took the plate but did not answer. Dub removed a large plastic container of fried chicken and three smaller ones filled with potato salad, cold slaw, and baked beans. A gallon-size resealable freezer bag of homemade hot rolls completed the meal.

"I thought maybe, this would be a good spot to start," Dub said as he handed her a fork and spoon.

"To start what?" She took them as he began to remove lids.

"To catch up." He placed a chicken breast on his plate before handing the container to her, "We spent a lot of time kicked back on this old gravel bar back in the day."

She nearly dropped the whole bowl of chicken, "What the

hell? Back in the day... back in the day... you mean back in the day before you broke my heart? Before you just up and disappeared and left me thinking I had done something wrong? Back in that day?"

"No," Dub pulled three serving spoons from the basket. "No, further back than that day. Back when you were my best friend. Back when we shared all our hopes and fears. Back when we really leaned on each other."

Not sure how to respond, she jerked a spoon out of his hand and used it to scoop potato salad onto her plate. He stuck a spoon in the coleslaw and used the remaining one to ladle baked beans onto his plate. Silently, the two filled their plates and began to eat. The soft gurgle of the creek flowing past slowly began to do its magic and even before she reached for a second piece of chicken a calmness had begun to work its way through her.

I may not much care for the asshole you are today, she thought, *but I do miss the friend you used to be.*

CHAPTER 11

"I was married for a long time." Katherine put her dirty plate on the blanket beside the picnic basket, laid back, crossed her arms behind her head, and stared up at the sky. "He cheated on me."

Dub used the last bite of a hot roll to sop up the bean juice on his plate. "I was married twice. Once for almost twenty-years."

"Did they cheat on you?" Katherine turned her head slightly towards him.

Dub put his plate on top of hers before answering, "I don't think so."

"Did you cheat on them?" Katherine's voice held a hint of judgement in it.

"No, I never did." Dub leaned back on his hands and stared out over the water. "I think the problem might have been that I was just an absentee husband."

"Absentee husband, what do you mean by that?" Katherine pushed herself back to a sitting position.

"I was gone most of the time." It took Dub some time to gather his thoughts. "And when I was home, I wasn't really there. At least not mentally. Looking back, I realize now that I wasn't much of a husband. I was a good soldier, a good Marine, but a good husband? No so much."

A frog added its call to the sound of nature's orchestra. It cut through the late afternoon air like the first sound of the steel guitar in an old country song. The soft murmur of the water flowing provided the background music as another frog responded. Somewhere further down the creek, a blue jay screamed.

"How 'bout you," Dub turned to look at her. "Were you ever unfaithful?"

"Never," Katherine answered and Dub had to smile at the indignation that rang heavy in her voice.

"I kind of figured." He glanced at her out of the corner of his eye.

Katherine's face had reddened, and he knew he was on shaky ground. "How so?"

"The Kat I remember wasn't that kind of person," Dub kept his voice low and soft. "I figured... well, I guess I hoped, that life hadn't changed that about her. I figured it hadn't, but I had to ask."

The sun had moved far enough west to leave the gravel bar in shadow and several insects had added their voices to that of the frogs' and birds'. While still not cool, the temperature had begun to drop. Dub waited for Katherine to respond. When she did not, he gathered up their dirty dishes and carried them to the edge of the creek.

The water felt good on his skin as he rinsed first the plates and then the silverware. Back at the blanket, he placed them in the bottom of the basket and then arranged the containers of leftover food on top of them.

"I thought maybe for dessert we'd swing through the drive thru for some ice cream," he suggested as he secured the top of the ice chest.

Katherine stood and picked up her shoes, "You promised no Dairy Queen. And besides if I add ice cream to the chicken and potato salad, I'll have to jog twice a day this week."

"You know Kat," Dub moved the Yeti and wicker basket off the blanket as he spoke, "if you worked half as hard at getting the bitterness out of your heart as you do at keeping the cellulite off your ass, you might be someone folks enjoyed being around."

Katherine's face flushed crimson, her eyes widened, and Dub had no doubt that if murder was not frowned upon, she would have beaten him to death with the heel of one the stilettoes she held. At first the words seemed to catch in her throat, and she made several sputtering sounds before she finally managed to get them out. "And if you weren't such an intolerable jackass, maybe people wouldn't have so much trouble being around you. What in the hell gives you the right to speak to me like that? What makes you think you know me at all? Oh, you arrogant, self-righteous, worthless... worthless..."

"Asshole." Dub finished the sentence for her.

"Yes," Katherine glared, "Asshole."

A grin spread across Dub's face. "I guess we both have some internal issues we need to work on, huh?"

Katherine's eyes narrowed, "Piss off." She managed before turning and starting towards the stairs that led back to the truck. Dub watched her until she reached the first step and then stooped down and gathered up the blanket. *Reckon I might have taken that one a little too far*, he thought to himself as he wadded the blanket around the food containers, *but all in all I think it's going fairly well.*

"The date did not go well," Mason's voice and the way he continued to tap a finger on the desk in front of him had begun to wear at Katherine's nerves. "At least that's what I believe your saying, Mrs. Taylor."

"Taylor... Taylor?!" Katherine's attempt to maintain a cool calm demeanor failed. "My name is Williams! His name is Taylor! I am not a Taylor! I am not Mrs. Taylor!"

Mason raised his both hands. "My apologizes, Mrs. Williams. I misspoke. It's been a long mornin'."

"Misspoke!" Katherine was not finished. "Misspoke! You ever call me by that jackass's name again, and you'll be lucky if you ever speak again!"

"Kat that's enough." Dub's voice cut through her tirade.

Her wrath turned from Mason to him in a split second, "Enough?! Enough?!" You have not seen enough. Dub Taylor you are coming very close to... to..."

68

"Deciding on a time for our next date." He finished the sentence for her.

"Next date... next date." Her inability to form a complete sentence only added to her frustration. "I'm not even sure I want another date."

"Seven o'clock this coming Tuesday," Dub continued as if they were having a causal everyday conversation, "I'll pick you up and we'll see a movie."

Katherine sat, teeth gritted, glaring at him. *He's winning again*, kept running through her mind like someone was playing it on an endless loop. She did not trust herself to speak and so rose from her seat and with a nod at Mason started for the door.

"Tuesday at seven o'clock then?" Dub said as she passed behind him.

She broke stride. "Dub Taylor, you can... you can..."

"Piss off?" Dub once again finished her sentence.

The thought of turning around and smacking him in the back of the head with her clutch crossed her mind, but her hand was already on the doorknob, so instead she opened it, stepped outside, and slammed it hard behind her. Halfway to her car, she realized she had not asked what she should wear on the date.

"Well, that went a little bit sideways." Dub grinned at Mason seconds after Katherine slammed the door.

"You think?" Mason was not smiling. "I don't know exactly what it is you're playing at Mr. Taylor, but I'd be careful how far I pushed that one."

The look on Dub's face grew serious and he rubbed the side of his jaw before he spoke, "You're probably right, there."

Mason took a pen from his shirt pocket and began to fiddle with it. When Dub did not stand or give any indication he was going to leave, Mason returned the pen to its place and asked, "Something on your mind?"

Dub ran a hand through his hair and leaned back. "I guess maybe we better talk about the seventh date."

"I think I'd be more worried about the third." Mason gave a chortle that ended in a snort, "Katherine looked mad clean through, I'm not so sure if Tuesday night is going to happen."

The grin returned to Dub's face. "Sure was pretty pissed wasn't she? I'm thinkin' maybe you might not want to call her Mrs. Taylor again."

Both men began to laugh and as the laughter continued, Mason could feel the tension from the meeting slowly melt away. The more he thought about the fit Katherine had thrown when he called her by Dub's last name, the harder he laughed and the harder he laughed the harder Dub laughed at him. After several minutes, Mason was wiping tears from his eyes. When the two finally got control of themselves, Dub said, "About that seventh date."

Mason took a box of tissues from the bottom drawer of his desk and wiped his eyes once more before speaking. "I'm guessing it's not going to be like the other six dates. There's going to be something a bit more significant to it."

"You might put it that way." Dub nodded.

Mason tossed the tissue he was using into a waste basket at the end of his desk. "Mr. Taylor," he cocked his head to the side as he spoke, "I hope, for your sake, you're not planning on trying to win her heart."

Dub chuckled. "Nope. That's not part of the plan."

"Care to share the plan with me?" Mason asked.

Dub held up a finger. "You know, now that I think about it, maybe we shouldn't get too far ahead of ourselves. Dad used to tell me not to count my chickens before the eggs hatched. I always hated it when he said it, but most of the time he was right and if he was here right now, I've a feelin' that would be his advice. Plus, you, yourself just illuminated the possibility that Kat might back out of Tuesday's date and if she was to do that, I guess the whole thing is off."

As much as the desire to know what his client had planned for the seventh date, Mason could not argue with Dub's logic and so nodded in agreement. Dub slapped his knee as if to say, *I guess that's decided then*, and rose to his feet. Mason stood and the two men shook hands before Dub started for the door.

As he settled his Stetson on his head, Dub looked back over his shoulder. "Guess I'll see you next Wednesday, one way or the other."

Mason echoed, "Until next Wednesday," as Dub went out the door.

Looking from the door to the file cabinet, Mason thought about the bottle of bourbon inside. The desire that normally surfaced at the end of a meeting was not there and he wondered why. He remembered reading somewhere that laughter helped release endorphins and in so doing helped improved your mood. Maybe that was the reason, he thought as he took the pen from his pocket, opened a desk drawer, and pulled out his appointment book.

Taylor/Williams-he wrote in the space for the following Wednesday beside the one o'clock time slot. "I wonder if they'll both show," He muttered to himself, as he closed the book and returned it to its place.

CHAPTER 12

Dub was not sure what kind of reception to expect when he put the truck in park and made his way to Katherine's front door. Halfway up the walk the door swung open and Katherine stepped out dressed in a pair of form-fitting gold lamé pants and a white beaded blouse. In one hand she carried her Louis Vuitton clutch and in the other a light-weight khaki-colored cardigan that matched her heels.

"I'm ready," she announced with a smile as she pulled the door shut behind her and strolled towards him.

Of all the possible scenarios he had formulated in his head over the last six days, this was not one he had anticipated. Anger, he was ready for, and the one he had figured most likely. Cold and aloof would have been his second guess. Katherine's carefree attitude and friendly smile had him stumped. She was a step past him before his brain rebooted and he had to hustle to try to get the door for her. To his surprise, she stepped aside and waited for him to open it.

"Thank you," she nodded pleasantly as she settled into her seat.

"You're welcome, my lady." Dub bowed slightly before shutting the door. *I wonder what she's playin' at*, he thought, *and how long it will last.*

As he made his way around to the driver's side of the truck, he found himself hoping they had reached a turning point. *Don't get too carried away there, soldier*, Sargeant Frye's voice warned, *and don't let your guard down.*

Katherine was well aware of the confusion her actions were causing. The only way it would have been clearer was if someone had written it across Dub's forehead in black Sharpie. Her visit with Jenn on Sunday had been very eye-opening. Without her daughter's help it would have never occurred to her to try this new tactic. Kind of an if-you-can't-beat-them-join-them maneuver, Jenn had called it. Katherine decided she liked it.

When Dub made a left at the end of her driveway instead of a right, she felt her newfound confidence waiver, and when less than two-hundred feet down the road, he turned into the lane that led to his house, she lost it altogether. The smile faded quickly, and she could feel her heartbeat quicken.

"I thought we were going to a movie," she managed to say as his home came into view.

She remembered the last time she had been here as a girl of sixteen. Dub's mother had met her on the front porch and explained that he was not seeing anyone. The pain had been unbearable and when the tears started to flow, his mother had wrapped her in her arms and tried to console her.

"We are," Dub assured her as he passed the house and pulled to a stop in the middle of a row of vehicles. "All the old drive-in movies are gone, so I decided to make my own."

"Oh my, Lord." Katherine felt like she was about to hyperventilate.

"Goodness, Kat," Dub's voice waivered. "Are you okay?"

Wide-eyed, she looked at the other vehicles and the people standing around them. She thought she recognized a couple of the men from town but could not be sure. In the years since her divorce, she had avoided town as much as possible, choosing a life of seclusion. It had taken all of her will power and quite a bit of encouragement from Jenn to prepare her for a movie amidst strangers with whom she would not be required to interact.

"I'm not sure I can do this," Katherine whispered. "I'm not good with people."

Dub reached over and took her hand. "You'll do just fine. It's just a few folks from church."

"I don't know." She shook her head.

With a smile, Dub patted her hand and said, "It'll be okay. You sit tight and I'll come around and get the door for you."

"You about ready to start this show?" Carl shouted from two cars away as Dub made his way to Katherine's door.

"Give us a couple of minutes." Dub hollered back, mentally kicking himself for not anticipating Katherine's anxiety. He had missed every sign, every red flag. Her refusing to acknowledge him the first time he had spoken to her at the mailbox. The way she nearly sprinted to the rear booth at the Dairy Queen and then sat with her back to everyone. She could be a little spitfire, but now he was beginning to realize that more than a couple of people to her was like kryptonite to the man of steel.

Dub opened Katherine's door and offered her his hand. She took it without a word. Instead of releasing her hand once she was clear of the truck, Dub guided it to his opposite elbow and then closed the door. Purposely he had placed her left hand on his right elbow, leaving her right hand free. She nodded and smiled as he introduced her to the five other couples in attendance. Greetings were exchanged and slowly Katherine's grip relaxed. Only Carl's wife offered a hand and Katherine took it without releasing her grip on Dub's arm.

"I think we've all got our seats set up." Kenneth waved a hand down the row of vehicles. "You need help getting ready?"

"I think I can manage," Dub said. "Carl do you have the projector all set and ready?"

"All I have to do is hit a button," Carl replied.

"Give us five minutes," Dub spoke over his shoulder as he guided Katherine towards the rear of the truck.

Dub dropped the tailgate, looked at Katherine, and realized

74

he had messed up. Dressed in his faded Wrangler's and a faded western work shirt, he was going to have no trouble climbing into the bed of the truck. Katherine, on the other hand, because of her choice of attire was not going to have such an easy time of it. *Didn't think this one all the way through, did ya, Marine*, Sargeant Frye's unwelcome voice chided. *Who's laughing now?*

"What the matter?" Katherine asked as he continued to look from her to truck.

"I maybe should have given you some guidance on your attire," Dub pointed at the cloth chairs lying beside the ice chest. "I had thought we would sit in the back of the truck while we watched the movie, but I don't think you can get up there in your outfit."

"Oh, I see." Katherine looked sheepishly around. "Once again, it seems I overdressed for the occasion, huh?"

"I'm sorry," Dub reddened. "I truly am."

"Y'all about ready down there?" Carl fussed with the angle of the projector resting on the tailgate of his truck.

To Dub's surprise, Katherine slipped her heels off and tossed them into the bed of the truck, "I'll need your knee," she said and motioned at the ground.

Dub quickly dropped to one knee. Katherine placed her hand on the side of the truck and stepped from the ground to his knee then from his knee onto the tailgate. Unaware that the other wives were watching, she blushed when they broke into a cheer. *If you can't beat them join them* popped into her head and with a flourish, she bent at the waist in a bow that brought on a round of applause.

"Just so you know," Katherine said as soon as Dub had her chair ready, "I still think you're a jackass."

Dub smiled, "Now there's the Kat I know."

"What movie are we watching?" she asked as he unfolded his chair and sat down.

"Hope Floats," he answered and then shouted to Carl, "We're ready whenever y'all are."

75

The projector came to life, illuminating the side of the old barn that sat behind the house. A large white sheet tacked to its side served as a screen.

"I don't really like this movie." Katherine's tone suggested a mixture of sadness and uncertainty.

"Have you ever watched it all the way through?" Dub opened the Yeti as he spoke.

"No," Katherine shook her head as Dub handed her a sweet tea. "I've never made it past the first part where... well, you know."

"Then you've never really gotten the movie's message." Dub shut the lid of the cooler and leaned back in his chair.

The movie's opening introduction began with a drum roll followed with blaring trumpets. Unlike the old drive-ins with their small individual speakers, the sound rolled across the yard from a massive sound system located below the makeshift screen. Even before the names of the leading actors and actresses began to flash across the old sheet, Katherine could feel her stomach twisting into knots. When the opening scene started, she feared she was going to vomit and she had a death grip on the arm of her chair.

Without taking his eyes off the movie, Dub reached over and placed his hand on hers and gave it a gentle squeeze. Almost as if some unknown force was guiding her, Katherine turned her hand over and laced her fingers with his and squeezed. As the scene unfolded, the main character's marriage was wrecked and the life she knew destroyed, Katherine felt long-buried emotions begin to surface. Her own divorce and the string of affairs that lead to it had caused a whirlwind of feelings she had never truly dealt with and so she had avoided this movie and any like it.

The plot moved forward, and Katherine eased her grip. It was if the writer had taken a page from her past and changed the names. There were differences of course. Her family had money and when she got finished with her ex-husband, she had a good portion of his to add to it. Her father had already passed, and her mother was living in an assisted care facility. Instead of moving back into the old home place, she saw to it that it was leveled and built her own place. But as she watched the movie and the effect the breakup had on the young girls in it, she realized how blessed she was that her children were grown and out of the house before her marriage went south.

Half an hour into the movie, Katherine watched the young female divorcee on the screen taking pictures with an old antique camera. As the actress developed photographs in a dark room, Katherine thought of her art classes in high school. She had loved to work with charcoal and pastels and had even tried her hand at a couple of oil paintings. She tried to remember why she had quit and could not.

The picture on the side of the barn froze and Carl hollered, "Intermission. Some of us need a restroom break."

Dub helped Katherine down from the bed of the truck and they walked to the back door of the house. After a brief discussion, it was decided that the ladies would use the facilities first and Dub gave directions to where the two bathrooms could be found.

"You okay, Kat?" Dub touched her elbow.

"I'm fine, Dub," she said and followed the other women into the house.

"I swear, it seems like I've got a bladder the size of a walnut and a prostate the size of an orange," Jim Lovett, owner of the local feed store, shifted from one leg to the other as the menfolk waited.

"I know what you mean," Kenneth laughed. "Seems like I spend more time standing over a toilet these days than anything else."

Pete Edwards, Dub's barber, and John Meade, a retired merchant, both nodded their agreement. Jim continued to shuffle around.

Dub looked from the door to his friends. "Unless you all need a sit down, I don't see why we can't step over to the edge of the yard. I don't reckon the ladies are gonna be out any time soon."

Everyone but Jim nodded their agreement. He was already crossing the lighted area towards the far end of where the trucks were parked.

"Haven't seen you at church in a while." John fell in beside Dub.

"Come to think of it," Pete chimed in, "we haven't seen you down our way in a while either."

Dub shrugged. "Just been makin' my way around. I'll get to you eventually."

"Don't know what you mean by around," Kenneth added, "but it's not the All-Faith Christian Church."

"Goodness, gracious," Dub chuckled. "You'd think by the way y'all are houndin' me, that I was the only sinner in town."

"Like any of us are saints," Kenneth huffed and the whole group shared a laugh.

At the edge of the light the five of them spread out in a line alongside Jim who was muttering something under his breath.

Katherine was just coming out of the second restroom, when Ida Manning who was washing her hands at the kitchen sink hollered, "Hey, y'all gotta see this. Get in here quick."

Katherine hurried into the room to find the others crowded around the window. The wives started giggling before she even had a chance to see what it was they were gawking at through the glass. Laura, Kenneth's wife, moved aside to make room for her. Her eyes widened and her first thought was to look away.

"Have you ever seen such a sight?" Faith Lovett shook her head.

At the very edge of the light, more silhouette than anything, the six men were standing legs spread urinating into the darkness. They were spaced evenly apart with their backs to the ladies completely unaware of the ruckus they were causing in the house.

"Lord, I'd give anything for a camera right now." Ida used her hands to frame the scene.

Katherine laughed. Where it came from she was not sure but it caused the others to start and before she knew it they were all wiping tears. Every time the laughter would start to die down, one of the women would snort and cause another bout.

Suddenly, still laughing, Ida clapped her hands. "They're done. They're done. They're comin' this way." She motioned them all back to the other end of the kitchen away from the window.

Gathered at the far end of the kitchen, Katherine noticed a pile of photographs lying between two stacks of shoeboxes. She stepped closer for a better look. The top picture was an old black and white of a young woman in a wedding dress. It took a minute before the face registered. It was Dub's mother. She was much younger than the woman Katherine remembered, of course, but there was no doubt in her mind that it was her.

She was considering looking at the rest of the pile when Carl eased the door opened and announced the men were ready, Ida suppressed a giggle before saying, "I thought you fellas needed to go."

"We already went." He shrugged and walked away leaving the door half open.

"You don't say?" Faith started in a very sophisticated ladylike tone then lost it as soon as the last word escaped her lips.

It took them several more minutes to compose themselves before they were able to join the men outside. On the way out the door, Laura reached out and touched Katherine's arm. When she turned, Laura smiled and said, "I'm sure glad you came tonight."

Katherine struggled for a second with a response but finally managed a thank you and a smile. A huge weight that she had not even realized was there seemed to rise off her shoulders and drift into the night air. For the first time in a very long time, she felt like she could breathe, really breathe. She was amazed at how such a simple act of kindness should be so freeing.

Dub helped her back up into the bed of the truck, Carl hit the button, and the movie continued. Katherine decided as she watched that the male character reminded her of Dub. Not in the way he looked, but in his persistence. The cowboy hat he wore helped quite a bit as well. When he asked the young woman to dance, she reached over and took Dub's hand. They spent the rest of the movie that way.

CHAPTER 13

The last goodbyes said, Dub stood beside Katherine and the two waved at the fading taillights. The light shining out through the kitchen window accompanied that from the crescent moon above and made long shadows across the yard. The sound of a pack of coyotes howling filled the night air.

"Guess it's about time to get you on home," Dub said, starting to dig truck keys out of his pocket.

"Not just yet. Let's sit and talk a little while." Katherine's response was so unexpected that Dub dropped the keys. As he bent to retrieve them, she added, "I have a couple of questions."

Now you've gone and done it, Sergeant Frye's voice accompanied the jangle of the keys as he stood up. Katherine had already started towards the back of the truck. Dub followed along and silently cussed the sergeant's unwanted commentary.

"Would you get the chairs down, please?" Katherine pointed up into the back of the truck. "I don't really want to have to climb back up there."

It took Dub only a minute to move both seats and the ice chest to the ground. He waited until Katherine was seated and had a fresh drink in her hand before sitting down himself. The coyotes had stopped howling and a couple of crickets out by the barn had started chirping. A barn owl hooted nearby. Dub sat patiently, listening to the night.

Katherine took a drink of sweet tea, screwed the top back on the bottle, and sat it on the ice chest. "First, I want to thank you for tonight."

Dub's heart leapt. "You're welcome."

"Second, just so we're clear," Katherine tapped a finger on the arm of her chair and continued, "I still think you're a jackass."

Dub chuckled.

"Now to the questions." Katherine's voice seemed both soft and stern. "Why?"

Dub waited for her to elaborate but she did not. When it became apparent that she did not intend to, he turned his head to look at her. "I'm gonna need a little more than that. Why what?"

Katherine shifted in her seat until her eyes met his. "Why did you insist on these dates?"

Dub filled his lungs with the cool night air and then let it out slowly. "That's a little complicated. Let me say first that it was not part of my plans when I came back to settle mom's estate."

"Complicated how?" Katherine picked up her tea bottle but did not open it.

"Do you recall the morning I stopped and spoke to you out by the road?" Dub nodded in the direction of Katherine's driveway. "Up by your mailbox."

"Yes." Katherine fidgeted a bit in her seat.

"I had seen you jogging out to pick up the mail on a couple of occasions." Dub paused and filtered his thoughts before continuing to speak. "I had mentioned your name in town and was told you had become... well a hermit."

"Something tells me more was said than just a hermit." Katherine cocked her head to the side and raised an eyebrow.

Dub chuckled. "And the phrase, bitter old woman, may have been used."

"I see," Katherine unscrewed the lid from her tea. "You may continue."

The barn owl hooted again, and the crickets grew quiet. The floral smell of her perfume drifted across the space between them. Dub breathed it in.

"I guess I needed to find out for myself if you were really as bitter as they said you were, so I stopped. Then you refused to speak to me." Dub made a sweeping motion with his arm. "As you know I was plannin' on donating it to the state. After you left, I went home and that's how it, well you know... the seven dates."

"But why?" Katherine leaned closer.

"Because I had to know if somewhere deep down inside a bitter old woman there was anything left of the beautiful carefree loving girl l once knew." Dub chanced a smile.

Katherine smiled back. "And why did you care one way or another?"

"The answer to that one is a bit selfish I'm afraid." Dub stared off into the night. "You see, I figured if I could find her, the girl, then there was hope for me."

"Hope?" the word hung between them for a long second.

"Yes, hope." Dub leaned his head back and stared up at the stars. "Kat, I've been lost for a very long time. So lost that I didn't even know I was lost. A few years ago, I picked up an old Bible and started reading it. And... I guess you could say I found the Lord. At least that's what most folks would say. I think perhaps it was the Lord who found me."

A lone coyote howled. The sad and mournful sound floated across the night. Dub stood and stretched. "The Lord found me even when I couldn't find myself. You see, Kat, the last time I felt like I really knew who I was, the last time I really even liked who I was, I was sitting on the tailgate of someone's truck in the middle of a pasture falling in love with the girl whose hand I was holding."

He looked down at her and smiled. He hoped the smile hid the heaviness in his heart as he offered his hand. She reached up, took it, and allowed him to help her to her feet. He pulled her close, moved the hand to his shoulder, and placed his free hand on her waist. As they danced in a slow circle to the sound of the crickets, she laid her head on his shoulder, and sighed. "You told me you weren't going to try to win my heart."

"I'm not tryin' to win it," Dub whispered, "I was just tryin' to see if you still had one."

"Jackass." Katherine chuckled.

"Bitter old hermit." Dub joked, and they both laughed.

Katherine spent the short drive from Dub's house to her front door, wishing the night did not have to end. When Dub put the truck in park and grabbed the door handle, she reached out and touched his arm. "I have another question."

Dub released the door handle and turned to face her. "Okay, let's hear it."

"Did you find her?" Katherine felt like a schoolgirl asking him if he liked her.

"I believe I did." One side of Dub's mouth turned up into a half smile.

Katherine felt herself blush. "You may not realize it… you may not be able to see it, but I do, or did. When you held me close tonight. When we were dancing, the Dub that stole my heart back in high school… I felt his presence. If that's the who you were looking for, don't give up hope, he's still there."

"You think so?" Dub looked doubtful.

"Yes, I do," Katherine reassured him, then added, "He may be hidden deep inside a sarcastic hardheaded old jackass, but he's there."

"Touche." Dub chucked. "Any more questions before I walk you to the door?"

"Maybe just one more," Katherine said, "It's getting late."

"Alright," Dub exaggerated a look at his watch. "Shoot."

"Did you really mean it when you said I need to spend more time on my spirit and less on my ass?" Katherine pooched her bottom lip out.

Dub clicked his tongue and shook a finger at her. "As usual, you weren't listenin'. I did not say you need to spend less time on your ass, I merely pointed out that you needed to spend more time on your spirit."

"Is that so?" Katherine pushed.

"It is." Dub's eyes sparkled. "It doesn't do any good to wash the outside of the dish, if the inside is dirty. Kind of defeats the purpose."

"Dub Taylor, how dare you use scripture on me." Katherine tucked her chin and rolled her head to one side. The shocked look on his face made her heart soar. "Yes, Dub, I know the Bible. I taught girls' Sunday school for years. Matthew twenty-three, verses twenty-five and twenty-six if I remember correctly."

"Well, I'll be damned." He laughed.

"You will indeed, if you ever say something like that to me again." Katherine hoped the stern look on her face made him realize she was serious. "Do we have an understanding?"

Still smiling, but head lowered, Dub looked at her with knowing eyes, and answered, "Yes, ma'am."

"Good. Now you can walk me to the door, you hardheaded old jackass." Katherine laughed.

As Dub opened the door, he laughed too. "You forgot sarcastic, my lady."

An hour later, Dub stood at the bathroom sink and stared at his reflection in the mirror. From the top of the towel he had wrapped around his waist, to the day's stubble that scratched at his neck, his body was lean, and his skin marred with more than a few scars. *Lookin' like you've lost a little ground there, soldier,* Sergeant Frye's chuckle echoed in his head. Dub smiled. It had been years since his abdomen had been well-defined enough to display the muscles, but for a man pushing sixty, he knew he was still in good shape. His eyes settled on a nine-inch scar that ran from the middle of his chest below his pec and disappeared under his arm. He ran a finger along it and the smile on his face vanished.

He closed his eyes and tried to think of something. Anything. But he had waited too long. Thought about it a second too long. Sergeant Frye's smiling face stared down into his. *You do not have my permission to die soldier! I did not drag your sorry ass out of that hell just to have you quit on me now, marine!* And then as it always did, the sniper's round found its mark and the center of the sergeant's face disappeared in an explosion of blood and brains.

Dub opened his eyes and gritted his teeth. He had lived. Again, he had lived, and another had died. And again, he had questioned God's judgement. Ben, Sergeant Frye, half his squad, all gone and somehow, for some unknown reason, God had seen fit to spare him. One of the many counselors he had seen over the years had once told him that time heals all wounds. He had come to realize that was absolute bullshit. Some wounds never heal. The best one can hope for is that they do not become septic to the soul.

He took a deep breath in, released it, and looked up into the eyes of his reflection. In the weeks following Frye's death, he had come about as close to losing his soul, and his mind, as a person can. And in the years that followed, he had done as much damage to the enemy as humanly possible, but he could not hate enough or kill enough to bring any of them back. Lord knows he tried.

He concentrated on the eyes, stared deep into those of the image in the mirror and tried to find the spirit Katherine claimed she had felt. Frustration welled in his eyes and clouded his vision. The still open wounds and the scars from battles past hid the boy from his view. It's the scars you can't see that cause the most damage and hurt the worst, he thought as he turned to leave the bathroom. Maybe the young man from his youth was in there somewhere. Maybe he would never know for sure, for now he would just have to be content to take Katherine's word for it.

CHAPTER 14

Mason Boyd could not have been more confused if Dub and Katherine had walked into his office dressed as circus clowns. The two had arrived at the door to his office simultaneously. Dub had held the door open. Katherine had smiled and thanked him. She had done everything but curtsy and Mason was beginning to wonder if they had ridden into town together. After the initial pleasantries, the two had all but ignored him.

A comment Dub made about seeing a cow out near the highway had sparked a conversation. Mason began to question if he had drunk too much the night before or perhaps, he had simply not consumed enough this morning. Whichever it was, he was beginning to believe miracles did occur.

Lord, I know I've asked you a number of times for a sign and promised to put down the bottle if you gave me one, Mason began a one-way conversation in his mind, *and this does seem pretty miraculous, but in my line of business I see temporary truces and momentary breaks in the battle fairly often, so I may need a little more convincing.*

"Mason, are you listening?" God's voice sounded an awful lot like Dub Taylor.

Mason refocused his attention with a shake of his head and looked at Dub. "Sorry, I kind of zoned out for a second there. You were saying?"

"Oh hell, Mason," Katherine cut in. "He was saying our fourth date will be next Wednesday. Lord have mercy, for what you lawyer's charge, one would think you could at least act like…"

"Now, Kat." Dub interrupted.

Mason braced for the storm he was sure she was about to unleash on Dub. When it did not come, he considered pinching himself to make sure the whole thing was not a dream.

"Well, shit Dub, he could..." Katherine rolled her eyes. "You're right, you're right, it's not my money. It's yours."

Too stunned to speak, Mason sat with his mouth hanging slightly open and looked from Dub to Katherine and back again. Katherine had turned her head and was glaring down the hall that led to the restroom. Dub gave an apologetic shrug. "Wednesday at six o'clock. Do you need to write that down somewhere?"

Mason pulled the pen from his pocket and reached for a notepad. "Fourth date, Wednesday. Got it. What day do you want to meet after the date?"

"Thursday works for me." Dub turned to Katherine. "Kat, that work for you?"

"If you think we need to keep meeting." Katherine's attitude was as confusing to Mason as her statement. "I'm fine with Thursday.

Twice Dub had called her Kat and still she had not retaliated. If it was not for the fact that she had nearly taken his head off, Mason feared he might have had to at least consider giving up his bourbon.

"Maybe, if it's not too much trouble, you could tell us what times you have available." Katherine's tone was neither warm nor friendly.

Mason did not even bother to look at his schedule. "Eleven o'clock," he quickly replied. In his mind he had already decided that if the time slot was already taken, he would call the other client, apologize, and reschedule them. A man could only handle so much. Dub and Katherine being civil to one another and now after the fit she had thrown two weeks ago, Katherine was questioning the need for the after-date appointments. Maybe God really was trying to give him a sign.

Friday evening after an early dinner of goulash and buttered bread, Dub sat down at the table and pulled the lid off the next box of photographs. Most of the second box had contained pictures of his mother and father's travels before his brother Ben was born. Towards the back, he had found pictures of Ben's birth and first year. Stuffed behind all the loose pictures he found a faded envelope. Inside it were the first images of himself. One of his mother holding him wrapped in a swaddling blanket, he had placed on the small pile he had started. The rest he had returned to the place he had found them.

Today's box, the third, with its yellowed tape label of 65 TO 70, was stuffed full of the paper envelopes that photographs come in when you pick them up after they have been developed. Dub pulled the first one out and found that written in the top right corner in his mother's handwriting was the month and year the pictures had been taken. Below that she had made a notation — Ben & Little Dub.

Inside he found twenty-four black and white prints. He took his time and looked at each photograph before placing it in the back of the stack. When he finished, he slipped them back into their envelope, slid it back into its place, and took out the one behind it. Slowly, methodically, one package at a time, he made his way to the back of the box.

None of the photographs did he add to his personal pile. He watched he and his brother grow from toddlers into school age kids as he worked his way through the box. He had no real recollections of any of the events in the photographs. The images were proof that he had been born and the first few years of his life had been filled with happy moments. He found himself wondering why people retained so few memories from their early years.

He secured the lid back in its place and stacked the box atop the first two. After a look at the red numbers on the microwave clock, he decided it was too late to start another box. He considered an unannounced visit to see Kat but Sergeant Frye's quelched the thought. *Easy there soldier. That's not part of the plan. Best to stick to the script.*

Irritated, he muttered an obscenity under his breath as he stood. The sarge was right of course, but that did not make it any easier to stomach. He stretched, stared down at the boxes one last time, and headed for bed. Maybe if he was lucky, he would be able to sleep tonight.

Sunday afternoon, Jenn made her way through the house looking for her mother. She was not in her bedroom, nor the sitting room. In the kitchen, Jenn found an open Bible on the bar. It was old and worn, and she thought perhaps it was the one her mother had used when she was in high school.

She peeked into the den and had just turned to check upstairs when she heard music in the game room. As she followed the sound, she recognized the singer as George Strait and the song was "Right or Wrong". At the archway between the two rooms, she stopped and stared in disbelief.

The pool table had been covered with a large gray tarp. The music was coming from her mother's cellphone which was propped at one end of the table out of harm's way. At the other end, her mother was swaying gently to the music and painting on a canvas she had setting on a short easel at the edge of the table.

When the song ended, before the next one began, Jenn cleared her throat loudly. "Who are you and what have you done with my mother?" she quipped.

Startled, Katherine flinched before turning to face her daughter. "Dammit, Jennifer Lynn, you scared the piss out of me."

Jenn laughed. "Really?"

"No not really." Katherine shook a paint brush at her.

"What in the hell are you doin' in here?" Jenn crossed the room and stood staring at the scene on canvas.

"What does it look like I'm doing?" Katherine smiled. "I'm painting."

Jenn could not take her eyes from the image. Six men, all in cowboy hats, spread out along a barbed-wire fence peeing. At first the scene shocked her into silence, but as she continued to take it in, she found the attention to detail and the quality of the work remarkable.

"Damn, mom, that is good." Katherine paused the music as Jenn spoke. "I'm not sure about your choice of subject matter, but the details. I didn't know you could paint."

"There's a lot of things you don't know about me." Katherine put her paintbrush into a coffee mug which had been placed alongside a plate filled with globs of different colors of paint and wiped her hands on the apron she was wearing.

A closer look and Jenn recognized the plate as one from her mother's good set of China. "I'm beginning to see that, mom." Jenn pointed at the ruined plate. "That was good China."

"Yes, it was." Katherine took a step back from the pool table to stand beside her daughter. "Now it's my palette."

Jenn moved her finger from the plate up to the canvas, "And that is a bunch of old men peeing."

"Yes, it is." Katherine laughed, "Isn't it wonderful."

"Not exactly the word I would have picked." Jenn looked from the painting to her mother. "What brought all this on?"

Jenn watched as her mother moved off to one side. Katherine continued to study the artwork and Jenn realized she had moved so she could see it from a different angle. Stepping back up to the table, Katherine swished the paintbrush around several times in the mug and then used a stained rag to wipe the bristles.

"Tuesday's date with Dub," she answered Jenn's question as she pulled the apron off and laid it on the edge of the table. "I think I'm finished, at least for today. Let's go fix a pot of coffee and visit."

91

Katherine sat a cup of coffee down in front of Jenn, closed the Bible and pushed it to the center of the bar, then seated herself. The smell of the fresh brewed coffee filled the kitchen as the two women waited for it to cool enough to drink. Katherine could feel the beginning of an ache between her shoulder blades. She had seen a sign somewhere that read, "Getting old isn't for sissies." She would have never imagined the simple act of painting would have taxed her muscles to the point of soreness.

"Mom, what happened to the driver who killed Dub's brother?" Jenn tried a sip of her coffee and found it still too warm.

Katherine considered telling Jenn she did not want to talk about it, but then decided it might be better to get it out. If she could not talk about it, how was she ever going to get past it? She had kept it bottled up way too long.

Katherine watched the steam rise from her coffee cup, "He was killed in the accident. I guess he saw Ben at the last minute and tried to swerve. The way it was explained to me was because of how fast he was going and how hard he turned, it caused the vehicle to roll several times. The car caught fire and he burned up in the flames."

"How awful." Jenn frowned.

"Yes, it was," Katherine agreed, "Two young men lost their lives that night. Three years later, Tim Jackson committed suicide. Remember me telling you about the guy with Ben that night?"

Jenn nodded.

"That was Tim. I guess he never really got over seeing it." Katherine looked over at her Bible. "It affected a lot of people, some more than others. I think too many of us didn't get the help we needed, and it changed our whole lives."

"I'm really sorry, Mom." Jenn reached out and patted her mother's hand.

"For what?" Katherine looked up at her. "You weren't even born."

"For bringing it up," Jenn said, "You were in such a good mood and now I've brought you down."

"Actually, in a way, if feels good to get it off my chest." Katherine placed a hand over her heart, "I think it has been buried in here too long."

Jenn took a sip from her cup, placed it back on the table, and pointed at the Bible. "That have anything to do with Tuesday's date?"

Katherine recognized her daughter's attempt to redirect the conversation. "You could say that."

"Care to elaborate?" Jenn raised an eyebrow.

"Not really." Katherine shook her head. "I will say this though, I feel different. Better than I've felt in years. Like maybe everything is going to be okay."

"That's great, Mom." Jenn smiled. "When's the next date?"

CHAPTER 15

Katherine refused to be suckered into overdressing a fourth time. She had pulled her hair into a messy bun, applied a little base and her favorite lipstick, and now stood in her closet and contemplated what she should wear. She knew the only answer she would get if she bothered to call Dub was the usual—clothes. The thought made her smile.

Dairy Queen, the dam for a picnic, and his house for a movie. She went over the past dates in her mind. That he had not given her a clue as to what this date might entail was a bit aggravating, but also a bit exciting. She decided to go for a working-on-the-spirit attitude and pulled a pair of worn faded denim jeans off their hanger. She had no trouble getting them on or zipping them up but when she stepped over to the mirror, she questioned how wide her butt looked.

Typical woman, Dub's voice whispered in the recess of her mind making her smile.

"I'll wear them to spite you then," she muttered under her breath.

She worked her way through her tops, sliding one piece of clothing at a time along the rail. From time to time, she would pull a hanger off and hold a bouse or shirt up against herself and check it in the mirror. After several minutes she found a t-shirt Jenn had bought her as a joke. It was pale pink and had never been worn. On one side of the front was the image of a knife buttering a homemade biscuit and beside it on the other side, printed in a fancy cursive stye was the phrase "You Butter Your Biscuits I'll Butter Mine & We'll Get Along Just Fine."

94

"Perfect." Katherine did not even bother to check it in the mirror but instead pulled it on and grabbed a pair of white Keds she used as loafers around the house. She had pulled the shoestrings out of them and since she had no idea what Dub had planned, she figured at least they would be comfortable.

Fully dressed, she brushed her teeth, touched up her makeup, and started to fix her hair. At the last second, she decided the messy bun went perfectly with her outfit and her attitude, and simply tucked a few wild stands in a tad tighter and left the bathroom.

The clock on her nightstand indicated it would be another thirty minutes before Dub arrived. She made a quick trip through the house to the game room. The painting was finished but something kept drawing her back to it. Something was missing.

Dressed in a long-sleeved, white, pearl snap shirt and pressed jeans, Dub pressed the button for the doorbell and waited. The thought that he should have told her the proper attire for the evening crossed his mind about the same time as Katherine opened the door. She stepped out and pulled the door closed behind her.

"Evenin', Kat." He stood and watched as her eyes traveled from his eyes down his frame to his ostrich-quill western boots.

"I hope those fancy shit-kickers don't mean you're planning on taking me dancing." She looked back up as she spoke.

Dub who had been reading her shirt, smiled, "Not at all, my lady. Are you ready?" And he offered her an elbow.

"Lead on, you ole jackass." She said and placed her hand on his arm.

Dub walked her to the truck and helped her in before he made his way around and got in himself. They had barely cleared the circle drive before Katherine spotted his Bible under the edge of the center console.

"You planning on preaching at me tonight?" She asked and pointed at the Good Book.

"Not hardly," Dub laughed. "I don't reckon I'm qualified."

"Didn't seem to stop you the other night." Katherine feigned indignation.

"All I did was paraphrase one verse," Dub argued. "You can hardly call that preaching. If I didn't know better, I'd think you were trying to start a fight with me."

Katherine gave him a sideways glance and then turned to look out the side window. Dub turned right out of her drive and five minutes later took a left towards Tishomingo. *Lord, are you sure about this?* Dub found himself asking as he drove. Sunday morning during church service he had asked for guidance on choosing a destination for this date. When he got the answer, he felt sure it was from the Lord, but now as he drew closer to town, he was not so confident.

Whether it was his wavering faith or if her own curiosity got the better of her, Dub did not know, but whichever it was, she turned and asked, "Just where are you taking me tonight?"

No guts, no glory, marine, Dub shook Sergeant Frye from his head, before he answered, "Church."

Katherine's mouth dropped open and she looked at him like he had just grown a second head. She began to stammer incoherently before her mouth slammed shut. She turned bright red, and her eyes widened.

Dub kept his eyes on the road ahead. "The All Faith Christian Church to be exact. Kenneth and Laura invited us."

"Us... Us?" Katherine barely managed to get the word out.

"Well, technically, they invited me, but seeing how it's date night, I figure the invitation extends to you as well." Dub continued to stare straight ahead.

"Dub Taylor, you are the worst kind of unbelievable... unbelievable..." Katherine continued to stammer.

Dub pulled to a stop at a redlight and looked at her, "Unbelievable?"

Katherine slapped his arm. "Unbelievable jackass!!"

Dub maintained a straight face as he spoke. "Now, Kat, is that any way for a lady to talk on her way to church?"

Katherine sat ramrod straight and stared out the window at the little white frame church in front of her. She was afraid if she looked down at what she was wearing she would break out in tears. So much for worrying more about what was inside than what was on her outside. If this was some sort of test, it was the hardest one she had faced so far. She wondered first if the land was worth it. Next it occurred to her that maybe she was no longer doing this just for the two hundred acres. And just before Dub opened her door, she thought, *then why the hell are you still doing it?*

The minute they walked into the sanctuary, Laura rushed over and grabbed her hand. "Paise the Lord," she threw up her free hand. "Oh, Katherine, I'm so glad you're here. Dub said you might come and here you are."

Katherine put her best smile on and mentally cursed Dub. Her eyes scanned the room as Laura continued to talk. Thankfully, there seemed to be only a few people in attendance. She wondered how early they were and how many more members would show up. In her peripheral vision, she could see Dub visiting with Kenneth a few feet away.

"Are you okay, Katherine?" The concern in Laura's voice caught her attention.

"Yes," she turned and looked at Laura. "I'm sorry, yes, I'm fine. Just a little out of sorts. Dub did not tell me we were going to be attending a church service."

"Oh, my," Laura scowled in Dub's direction, "that wasn't very nice of him."

Dub, who was lost in conversation, did not notice.

"No, it was not," Katherine agreed. "I would have dressed for the occasion had I known."

Laura looked Katherine over and then giggled. "Wednesday nights are casual. Some of our members get dressed up for the Sunday mornin' service, but not everyone. Still Dub should have let you know." She wrapped an arm around Katherine shoulders, glared at the back of Dub's head and whispered, "Men can be such asses, can't they?"

A gasp escaped from Katherine and then a giggle. "Laura."

"What?" Laura shrugged, "Ass is in the Bible."

"So it is." Katherine could feel the tension beginning to leave her body.

"There's someone I want you to meet." Laura started down the center aisle, arm still around Katherine's shoulders. Katherine let her guide her towards the pulpit. As the two women made their way forward, Katherine noticed a head turn here and there. She was glad that no one seemed to be gawking. It seemed to her that the members were simply seeing who was passing before turning back to their conversations. She felt a bit more comfortable, if not completely at ease, but decided she was still angry with Dub.

An elderly man Katherine figured must be nearing eighty stood talking to a woman seated in the first pew. When Laura and Katherine drew near, he looked up and his mouth widened into a huge smile. Katherine could not ever remember seeing a face that held more kindness or that made her feel so cared for and she could not help but return the smile.

"Brother Jerry, this is Katherine. Katherine, this is Brother Jerry." Laura introduced them, "He is our pastor."

"It's so nice to have you here." Brother Jerry reached out and took Katherine's hand. "Let me introduce you to my wife." He smiled down at the woman he had been visiting with. "This is Vivian."

Vivian turned to look up at her and smiled. "Oh, how wonderful. We're so glad you're here. Please, excuse me if I don't stand. I broke my ankle last week."

"It's nice to meet both of you." Katherine hoped she did not sound too formal. "And I'm glad to be here." It came out before she could think but as soon as it did, she realized it was the truth. She really was glad to be there.

"Laura and Kenneth tell us you used to teach Sunday school." Vivian patted the pew beside her. "Sit with me a minute."

Laura took her arm from around Katherine and the two settled in beside Vivian. Brother Jerry gave the three a knowing smile and drifted away.

"Our little church is growing." Vivian placed a wrinkled hand on Katherine's knee. "Our morning Bible study has grown so big that we have discussed splitting our women's devotional up, but no one has the time needed to prepare for and lead the second class. We were hoping you might be interested."

Katherine was speechless. She looked from Vivian to Laura, who was all smiles.

"Of course, you don't have to decide right now." Vivian patted her knee. "You enjoy the service and then maybe we can talk afterwards."

Katherine managed, "Yes, ma'am," but could not seem to verbalize anything more.

"Good." Vivian patted her once more before Laura stood up and grabbed her hand again. She led her back to where Dub and Kenneth were still visiting, gave Dub a stern look, took Kenneth by the arm, and led him away without saying a word.

Dub turned to Katherine, smiled, and nodded towards a pew. "Let's sit over there."

A whirlwind of emotions was creating a mental tornado in Katherine's chest and head. She wanted to scream at Dub. The thought of slapping the smile from his face flew across her psyche like rubble in an Oklahoma twister. Her brain flashed a gigantic *You're In Church* sign or she might well have carried out the impulse. Delighted at being asked to teach a Sunday school class and the joy of how accepted she felt meshed with the anger.

The anger began to fade as consideration began and a mental argument ensued. She had taught before; she could do it again.

Fear took over. It had been too long. She had drifted too far from God. Determination fought its way front and center and as Brother Jerry stepped to the pulpit, peace and hope settled in.

The service lasted an hour. There was a time of prayer, followed by announcements, then the congregation sang hymns of praise before the pastor gave his sermon. Katherine sang along with the hymns and tried to listen to the message, but her mind would not settle enough for her to do it. When the congregation was dismissed after a final prayer, she could not even remember what part of the Bible had been preached from, but she knew she had found a place of peace. A place she had not searched for but had needed badly.

Several members introduced themselves as they passed her and Dub on their way out. She smiled and did her best to catalog their names for future reference. One of the wives even told her she loved her shirt.

At the door Brother Jerry stopped them. "I hope you enjoyed the service."

"As always." Dub nodded.

"And I hope my lovely wife did not scare you off." He turned to Katherine.

"Be right outside," Dub said and walked away leaving her and Brother Jerry to talk alone.

"No, sir." Katherine smiled. "I very much enjoyed being here tonight."

"Wonderful." Brother Jerry pressed his palms together in front of his chest and for a second Katherine thought he was about to pray. "That is just wonderful, and I hope you will at least consider helping us. Vivian has a way of... well, let's just say she's a very good judge of character and if she liked you enough to ask you to lead a class then I have no doubt you will do a marvelous job."

"Brother Jerry," Katherine could feel the slow steady beat of her heart as she replied, "It has been a long time since I led a devotional, as a matter of fact, it has been a long time since I've even set foot in a church. I am not sure my spirit is in the right place. I would like to sleep on it and pray about it."

"I would be disappointed if you didn't." He smiled. "That statement tells me your spirit is heading in the right direction, and Katherine, none of our spirits are in the right place but if we are following the Lord our spirits are headed in the right direction. When you get an answer from God, you let me know. There is no hurry."

"Thank you so much." Katherine wanted to hug him but did not.

As she turned to go, Brother Jerry said, "Oh, and Katherine, please don't be too hard on Dub. His actions might be questionable, but his heart is in the right place."

CHAPTER 16

Dub watched Katherine as she crossed the parking area. The girl he had known had grown into a beautiful woman. He had seen that the first day he had seen her at the mailbox. The woman walking towards him tonight was even more gorgeous. Whatever he had coming, and he knew there would definitely be something, he would gladly take it. Whether she ever set foot inside this church, or any other church again, tonight she looked at peace. The weight that had held her down, that had hidden the young lady from his youth, was gone. He knew there was no guarantee it would not return, but at least tonight, she was free of it, and he found himself hoping the freedom was forever.

"You are an ass and that's all I have to say to you." Katherine walked past him and stood by the passenger door.

"Yes, my lady." Dub opened the door and bowed.

Katherine did not respond. She did not even look his way. She still had not spoken when Dub turned up her drive. He had just about decided he would prefer a good cussing instead of the silent treatment when she turned sideways in her seat and pulled her feet up against her bottom.

"I think you may be the biggest ass I've ever met," she began.

"I'm..." Dub started to speak.

"Oh, no you don't," Katherine cut him off. "Oh, no you don't. It's my turn to talk. You just drive and listen, buddy. First off, that is the last time we go anywhere without me knowing how to dress for the occasion. If it happens again, I will kick your sorry ass and by all that is holy, you will let me. Secondly, I am mad at you, and it may take me a while before I get over it."

Dub pulled to a stop, put the truck in park, and sat quietly.

"And lastly, and most importantly, thank you for taking me to church tonight. I found something there that I lost a long time ago."

Dub felt a smile playing at the corner of his mouth.

"If you smile, I swear I will punch you." Katherine turned quickly in her seat and reached for the door handle. "I will get out myself, I don't need your help. You just watch me to the door and then get the hell off my property."

As he watched her step down, Dub figured she was going to slam the truck door. To his surprise, she did not. As instructed, he watched to make sure she was safely inside before driving away. When he passed the mailbox, he began to chuckle. He was still laughing when he pulled to a stop in his own drive.

Katherine made her way through the house to her bathroom. She turned on the water in the garden tub, adjusted the temperature, added scented bubbles, and while it filled she removed her makeup and undressed. The muscles between her shoulder blades reminded her that she had overdone it with the painting and now that she was alone the tension, like a rubber band that had held her together, had been pulled too taunt and snapped. She felt it first in her chest. Her shoulders began to quiver and before she could stop it, she began to bawl. Not cry. This was not simply tears running down her cheeks. This was soul-cleansing, gut-wrenching sobs that shook her body to the core. She did not try to control it. She let it go, let it consume her, until after nearly a half an hour it played itself out.

Halfway through it, she turned off the water. When it ended, she eased herself down through the bubbles and into the bath. The water was hot enough to make her skin tingle and the scent of lavender filled the air. She closed her eyes and listened to the sound of the bubbles popping. Completely spent, she felt a peace she had not known existed.

A memory of her mother's face floated across the back of her eyelids. Soap suds in the kitchen sink slid off the plate Momma had just washed as she handed it to Katherine. If she concentrated, Katherine could smell the floral scent of her mother's perfume.

"If you're sad, it's okay to cry, you know," her mother was saying, "It's not good to hold it in. A good cry cleans the soul and heals the heart."

Katherine opened her eyes and softly whispered, "You were right, Momma."

Dub wandered through the house aimlessly. The restlessness was something he had grown attuned to and tonight all the signs of insomnia were present. It had taken him years to come to terms with the idea that his leaving had hurt Katherine. The hole the revelation had left in his heart had never completely healed. Somewhere along the way he had acclimated to it, but tonight he found himself struggling with the knowledge that she was upset with him again.

He needed something to take his mind off her. In the kitchen the boxes of pictures caught his eye. They were not what he really wanted to do tonight. They were, however, a distraction. He pulled out his chair and sat down.

The fourth box—71 TO 73—was next. Seventy-one was the year he had turned seven. The year he had peed on Katherine. The first day he could recall where he had felt like his brother's shadow. It had made him angry. Youth and anger are never a good combination.

It had started innocently enough with Ben, who was eight at the time, suggesting a game of hide-and-seek. Katherine and her older sister Vickie had gotten permission to come to their house and as usual Ben and Vickie, who were just a few months apart in age, had been bossing Dub and Katherine around most of the morning. Ben decided they should draw straws to decide who was it. Dub had drawn the short straw. Tired of being told what to do, he had thrown the straw down and stomped over to the tree where he was supposed to count.

"Why are you actin' like a little brat?" Vickie had snarled, "It was a fair draw. Quit bein' a baby."

Even now all these years later, Dub could feel the tension drawing his shoulders up and he had to stop himself from clenching his jaw. It was crazy that the memory of that day could still have such an effect on him. He knew it was because he still struggled with the thought that he had always played second fiddle to his brother. Even after his death, Ben's memory seemed to overshadow him. For years he had told himself it was all in his mind. There were even times he had managed to convince himself that it was not real, just his own insecurities. Even if it was true, it still did not make it hurt any less.

"One, two, three..." He had counted slowly to fifty. When he had turned around, he was seething. In his seven-year-old mind, the game was no longer about finding Vickie, it was about revenge. No one was going to call him a brat and a baby and not pay for it.

The barn had been old even back then. With several outbuildings and a couple of old metal grain silos out behind, it had lots of places to hide. That day, Dub figured Ben would be in his favorite hiding place up in the hayloft. Ben, he could care less about. In Dub's mind, Ben should have defended him, but he would deal with that later. The mission in front of him was Vickie.

Dub had stepped to the barn door and hollered, "Ready or not here I come."

Then the search had begun. At the back of the barn someone had built two stalls. At some point in time, they had been used to house horses. For years, an old leather harness, brittle with age had hung on a rusty nail beside the corner stall. One of the horses kept there must have been a kicker because sections of boards were missing down low on both the side and the back of the barn. As Dub eased along looking for Vickie, he saw a set of skinny little legs through the opening left where the horse had kicked a board away.

Looking around to make sure no one was watching, he had unzipped his pants and peed through the opening on the back of what he thought was Vickie's legs. The legs turned out to be Katherine's. He had received the worst whipping of his life after which he was made to apologize to her in front of everyone.

"I'm sorry I peed on you," Dub remembered saying. "I thought you were Vickie."

Dub pulled the box of pictures across the table and took the lid off. He picked the first envelope of photographs out still thinking about that day. Vickie had never really liked him after that day and to be fair, the feeling was mutual.

The fifth package of pictures he opened were in color. When he finished looking at the last set of pictures and placed the lid back in place, he had two piles of pictures on the table in front him. He had added a few to his original stack. The ones he planned to take with him. Beside that one, he had started a pile of pictures for Katherine. He had been surprised when he began to find photographs which included images of Katherine or Vickie and sometimes both. He did not know why it had come as such a shock that they would be there, after all, they had practically grown up together. Still as the pile had grown, the memories from those years had slowly begun to fill his mind. By the time he placed the box on top of the others he had already gone through, he was exhausted and ready for sleep.

Half an hour later, after a quick shower, he stretched out in the bed and closed his eyes. *I wonder how long she's gonna be upset with me this time*, was the last thought that passed through his mind before he slipped off to sleep.

Three-quarters of a mile away, Katherine wandered aimlessly from room to room. Mentally, emotionally, and spiritually exhausted, she wanted only to lie down and sleep, but her brain refused to allow itself to be shut off. Standing in one of the four upstairs rooms, she began to question her need for such a big house.

Perhaps it would be different if her children lived close and visited more often. Jenn of course came around, but she was single with no children and she did not seem to be in any hurry to get remarried. Ashley, her older daughter and middle child, was married with two children, a boy and a girl. They visited a couple of times a month on the phone, but she lived in Virginia where her husband's job kept him busy and had not been out in nearly two years. And then there was her son, Robert John McClary III, R.J. to his family and friends. He was the spitting image of his father and though Katherine loved him, she found it hard to be around him. Not only did he resemble his father, but he had also adopted his father's womanizing ways. Two divorces behind him, the last time he had visited he had brought his fiancé. When they had left, Katherine had felt sorry for the young woman and had for days been filled with regret at not having warned the girl about her son.

She tried to remember what had possessed her to build such a big house. Frustration, pride, and anger all came to mind. A scorned woman and anger are never a good combination, she thought as she left the room and made her way back to the first floor. She was afraid this was never going to be the home her heart wanted.

Back in her bedroom, she stretched out and thought about the Sunday school position she had been offered. Life seemed to be throwing a lot at her all at once. It was as if her hermit life had been a dam and by allowing just a little water to flow around the edge of it, she had inadvertently caused a flood. Sink or swim, Jenn's voice rang out in her head.

Tomorrow. Tomorrow she would decide. A decision about church, about the house, about what she wanted to do with her life. Tonight, she had decided to live again, and that was enough for one evening.

Thank you, Dub, she smiled as she drifted off to sleep, *and in case you're wondering, I'm still angry with you, but I'll get over it.*

CHAPTER 17

Mason was glad he had not given up drinking as he sat across from Dub and Katherine. If there was such a thing as a rewind button in one's life, Mason felt like someone had used his. It was like last week's meeting had been a dream and reality was sitting in front of him this morning.

Katherine would speak to Mason. Mason would repeat what she said to Dub, who would then respond by speaking to Katherine. Katherine would then ignore Dub and respond to Mason. Had he been watching the scene in a movie, Mason was sure he would have seen the humor in it, however, being a part of it in real life was not nearly as funny.

"I would like to know exactly what the plan is for date number five." Katherine looked at Mason across the desk.

When he was sure she was finished speaking, Mason turned to Dub, "Mr. Taylor what are your plans for date number five?"

"Carl was telling me about this little place over by Lake Texoma called Ollie's Juke Joint & Café. It's the other side of Kingston and he said the food is wonderful." Dub had his head turned and was talking to Katherine, but from time to time he glanced Mason's way. "I figured I'd pick you up around four thirty and we'd drive over and check it out. Sometimes they have live music, but I'm not sure if they will next Thursday."

"So next Thursday at four thirty?" Mason made a note on his pad.

"Dinner at Ollie's." Dub repeated the destination and Mason added it to his notes.

"We'll meet back here the Friday after, let's say at one o'clock." When he had finished writing, Mason looked back to Katherine, "Is there anything else you would like to know?"

"The appropriate attire for the evening?" Katherine turned to glare at Dub. It was the first time she had even acknowledged his existence since he had walked through the door.

"Fair enough." Dub nodded, "Casual. I'm gonna wear jeans and a shirt. Probably won't even bother to polish my boots."

Katherine turned back to Mason once again ignoring Dub. "That is all I need to know."

The tension in the room was thick enough that for a second Mason thought he might be able to grab a handful. In all his years of practicing law, he had never been happier to feel a room so full of hostility. Unlike last week, this felt normal. It felt right.

"How about you, Mr. Taylor," Mason glanced at Dub, "are you satisfied?"

Dub reached out and placed an envelope on the desk in front of Katherine. "I'm good," he said to Mason and then turned to Katherine. "I found these among some of mother's things and thought you should have them, Kat."

As she reached to pick the envelope up, Dub stood and started for the door. Mason watched Katherine open the packet, look inside, and then close it back. Before she did, Mason caught a quick glimpse of the photographs inside. The sound of the door closing let him know Dub had left. Katherine sat very still for several seconds before placing the pictures into her purse. Mason was not sure but as she turned to leave, he thought he saw tears beginning to well up in her eyes.

Dub drove past the house and barn. The old ruts that started between the two silos and ran off out into the pasture were nearly grown up. He eased along and watched for any places that might have washed out. As he neared the far back corner of his land, he pulled to a stop. In years past, his father would yearly sow a few acres of rye to attract deer.

It had been years since the last rye had been sowed. The native vegetation had reclaimed the old plot. Dub stepped out of his truck and walked out across the field. The Tishomingo National Wildlife Refuge was just across the fence and often in the evenings deer could be seen foraging in the open area where the old plots had once been. Dub did not expect to see any this early in the day, but deer were not the reason he had driven out anyway.

He reached into the pocket of his shirt and pulled out an old photograph. It had been taken by his mother from the bed of his father's truck. Katherine had wanted to see the deer. After getting permission from her parents, Dub's mother had driven he and Katherine out to this very spot. He tried to remember why his dad and Ben had not been with them but could not.

Just as the sun dropped over the edge of the horizon, his mother had stood in the bed of the truck against the cab and instructed Dub and Katherine to stand on the tailgate. His mother had snapped a couple of pictures and then told them to stand closer together. Dub had reluctantly moved close, and Katherine had unexpectedly put her hand around his waist. Not knowing what to do with his arm, he had draped it over her shoulder. The photograph that his mother had snapped, he now held out in front of him.

He had found it in the last box of pictures he had gone through. His mother had not shown it to him when it had been processed those many years ago. The smile on Katherine's face and the confused blush on his was both comical and sweet. The deer feeding in the background somehow added an element of innocence. It was the first time he remembered feeling anything for anyone outside of his family. Some might have called it love, but Dub knew it had not really been love. In his mind it had been the seed that one day would have grown into love if the accident had not happened.

He stood for a long time looking at the photograph against its original background. He worked hard to memorize every detail in it. Katherine's smile, the sparkle in her eyes, the way her hand wrapped around his waist, and the way his hand hung awkwardly over her shoulder, all of these he tried to commit to memory. When he could concentrate no longer, he put it back into his pocket, and returned to his truck.

The trip back to the house seemed to take longer than the trip out and he smiled to himself. It reminded him how easy it was to run away and how hard and how long it took to return. He wondered if he had known this as a young man, if he would have chosen more carefully. His thoughts turned to Katherine. He decided if do-overs were possible, he would definitely do things differently.

Katherine parked her car in front of the All Faith Christian Church, got out, and went inside. She found Brother Jerry on a ladder behind the pulpit changing a lightbulb. She walked down the center aisle of the sanctuary with her head high and her eyes forward. Brother Jerry had just started down the ladder when she reached the front.

"Hello, Katherine," he said as he stepped off the last rung. "It's good to see you this afternoon."

"I am here to tell you I would be honored to take the Sunday school class you offered." The words spilled out of her mouth so quickly that she surprised herself. "That is, if it is still available."

Brother Jerry smiled. "It is and I've been expecting you."

"How is that?" Katherine frowned. "I told no one."

Brother Jerry handed her the lightbulb he had been holding. "I have my ways." He grinned and glanced up at the ceiling.

Katherine followed his eyes up and then his reference to the Lord registered and she blushed. When she looked back to the pastor, he had folded the ladder.

"Let me put this away and then we'll step over to the parsonage." He moved as he spoke. "Vivian will be the one for you to talk to about the class."

Katherine followed him down a short hallway to a storage closet. He sat the ladder inside and the two of them stepped through a side door and crossed the short distance to the parsonage. Brother Jerry held the door open to allow Katherine to enter first. As he entered, he announced, "Vivian we've got company, but you sit tight and we'll come to you."

The home was clean and tidy. Katherine noticed several pictures of what she figured were the couple's children and their families. A few knickknacks on a small wooden shelf spoke to the simplicity of the home. There was nothing one would consider fancy about their decorations or their furnishings. Humility and servitude were visible everywhere she looked.

"Oh, I'm so glad you came back." Vivian laid the Bible she had been reading aside on the arm of the couch where she was sitting and reached her hand out to Katherine.

"Thank you, ma'am." Katherine took the offered hand and allowed herself to be guided onto the cushion beside Vivian.

"She's decided to lead the class." Brother Jerry smiled. "I told you not to worry and that she would be back, now, didn't I?"

Vivian rolled her eyes at Katherine and then looked up at him. "And so you did, and I'm sure you're awful pleased with yourself, but now Katherine and I need a little time, so if you'll go get yourself ready..." She waved a hand to shoo him along, then turned to Katherine, "I have a doctor's appointment in a little bit, but we can visit while he gets around."

Katherine could hear Brother Jerry chuckling as he disappeared. Vivian began to tell her what chapters the women's group had been studying. Katherine breathed deep. She could not remember a time when things felt this right.

The picture of his mother Dub placed on the table by itself. Beside it he laid the small stack he planned to take with him when he left. On the top was the picture of Katherine and him. Why it gave him courage, he did not know, but the remaining four boxes no longer caused him despair. He looked once more at the photograph with the deer in the background and then took the fifth box from the second stack and removed its lid.

Only two years' worth of envelopes—74 & 75—printed on the worn tape. The first package held images from his first little league baseball game. Ben had been playing for two years by then but Dub had not really been interested in sports. That all changed that summer. He finally found something he was better at than Ben and baseball became his favorite sport. He loved it. Ben hated it.

Over half of the envelopes in the box were packages of Ben or him, or both playing one sport or another. One set of prints were of him at a basketball game. He laughed aloud at his ten-year-old self. The boy in the photographs, with spindly legs and a skinny torso, reminded him of a three-day-old colt. Basketball had not been his game and it was the only year he had played. After that he left the court to Ben and stuck with baseball and later football.

In the packets that did not hold sports photographs, Dub found a handful of pictures that included Katherine and two that had Vickie in them. All of them were taken around the old barn except for one, and this one his mother had taken without either he or Katherine's knowledge. How she had managed would forever be a mystery. The image was of him pushing Katherine on an old rope swing that had once hung from the big elm tree behind the house. From the angle, Dub could tell it had most likely been taken from the back porch. The timing had to have been perfect. In the image, on the return the swing had reached its peak. A young Dub stood on tiptoes with the edge of the wooden seat in his hands. Katherine had her head thrown back and to one side and was laughing. Somehow the shutter had opened at the exact instant the swing stopped because the image was flawless.

Dub held the photograph in his hand for a long time before he laid it down on the stack he had made for himself. He put the lid back on the box and moved it to the end of the table with the other four he had already looked through. He considered starting another box and decided against it.

With the newly found picture in hand, he made his way to the back porch. As he had done earlier in the day, he held it in front of himself against its original background and did his best to memorize it. The old rope swing had long since disappeared. He could not remember the last time he had seen it, but he found himself wishing it was still hanging there as the setting sun turned the horizon behind the old tree bright shades of orange and red.

Katherine sat on a lounge chair beside the swimming pool and watched the sunset color the sky. Once the last sliver of the huge red circle disappeared below the horizon and the golden hour started, she picked up the stack of pictures she had laid on the little table beside her. She had already looked through them a few times before laying them aside and picking up her Bible.

Now with the Good Book stretched across her lap, she slowly flipped through them again. There were a couple of her and Vickie together. Neither of them looked happy in the pictures. It occurred to her that they had never really liked each other much and she wondered why. Perhaps it was that Vickie had always had the attitude of an only child or maybe because she had always resented the attention her parents, especially her father, had given to Vickie. Whatever the reason, she suddenly found herself adding a better relationship with her sister to the long list of things she needed to do that she had begun to compile in her head.

She slid the photograph of her and Vickie to the back and sat staring at one of her and Dub standing on the tailgate of his father's old truck. She remembered the day it had been taken. The deer in the background made her smile and then she recalled Dub's mother asking them to move closer together. She flipped through the next couple of pictures but did not find the image she was looking for and wondered where it might be.

She shivered, blamed it on the night air, and gathered the pictures and her Bible. As she rose from her seat, her conscious corrected her, and she knew the memory of Dub's arm around her shoulder and the feel of him close had caused the shiver. The smile that spread across her face reached a new depth and for the first time in years her heart smiled.

CHAPTER 18

"Ollie's Juke Joint & Café," Jenn repeated what her mother had said. "Sounds like a fun place."

She had arrived for her usual Sunday afternoon visit to find her mother just getting home from church. Katherine had dropped her Bible and purse on the bar and asked Jenn if she had eaten. She had not and it was decided they would have sandwiches and chips for lunch.

"I guess so." Katherine took a package of sliced cheese from the fridge and placed it on the bar with the lunch meat and mustard which were already there. "Grab the bread from the pantry, please."

"And when is this date going to happen?" Jenn asked over her shoulder as she opened the pantry door.

"Thursday evening," Katherine answered as she added lettuce and tomatoes to the collection of items on the bar. "Do you want onions? I can slice some if you do."

"Only if you do." Jenn laid a loaf of white bread down. "So did you go to church with Mr. Taylor this mornin'?"

Katherine had taken an onion to the sink and was peeling it over the garbage disposal. She rinsed it off, pushed the outer layer down out of sight, and flipped the switch. After several seconds, she turned it and then the water off, and turned back to the bar. "No, I went by myself. I didn't see Dub there. I guess he stayed home or went to another church."

"Which church did you go to?" Jenn took plates down from the cabinet while Katherine sliced a tomato and the onion.

117

"The one Dub took me to." Katherine cored the head of lettuce. "The All Faith Christian Church, you know the little white one across the creek."

Jenn set the plates on the bar. "Is that not the one Dub attends?"

Katherine gave her an I-really-don't-know look. "That's a good question."

Jenn handed her mother one of the plates and both women fell silent as they fixed their sandwiches. The smell of fresh cut onions and tomatoes filled the room. Jenn loved it. The clink of the knife against the side of the mustard jar added a momentary clatter to the crinkle of a plastic wrapper being removed from a slice of cheese. For some, home was where the heart was, but for Jenn, home was where the food was, and it did not have to be fancy. She remembered a time when Sunday afternoon was synonymous with fried chicken and homemade hot rolls. Those times had also been filled with a lot of tension and anxiety. If this new atmosphere of peace and joy meant she had to live on sandwiches, well then, Jenn decided she was just fine with it. Bring on the ham and cheese.

"Mom, how did Aunt Vickie take it when Dub's brother died?" Jenn asked her mother between bites.

Katherine finished chewing the bite of sandwich in her mouth, swallowed, and took a drink. "I would say she used it to her benefit."

"What do you mean by that?" Jenn sat her sweet tea down and waited as her mother took a drink of hers.

"Your Aunt Vickie took after my dad," Katherine explained. "Now I loved my dad and I love Vickie, but they may be the coldest two people I've ever been around. Some people are loving, and some are not, but Vickie took the not to a whole other level. Also, Vickie has always been stuck on herself... mmm, or you could say she thought very highly of herself. I think that is why her and Ben were always fighting. He thought highly of himself too. Anyway, when he died, she went into the poor pitiful girlfriend routine, at least out in public, but at home she acted like she could care less. Shortly after the accident, I even caught her talking to a guy from Madill. When I questioned her about it, she told me to mind my own business."

Jenn studied her mother's face and wondered if this was just more of the bitter rivalry that Katherine and her aunt had shown for as long as she could remember. The usual narrowed eyes and slightly curled lips that Katherine usually had when she talked about Jenn's aunt were not there. Katherine spoke as if she was talking about the latest weather. Jenn found it odd that her mother seemed so calm, not just when talking about her Aunt Vickie, but about everything.

Changing the subject, Jenn picked up her sandwich as she spoke. "So, Ollie's on Thursday. Are you excited about this date?"

"I don't know that excited is the correct word," Katherine picked up her sandwich. "but I'm okay with going."

"You're not falling in love with Mr. Taylor, now are you, Mom?" Jenn kidded.

The sandwich which had almost reached her mother's mouth stopped. Katherine looked at her from under her brows. "You're not too old to have your mouth washed out with soap, young lady."

After the Wednesday night service at the First United Methodist Church, Carl caught Dub as he was about to leave. Dub had just sat down and placed his Bible in the passenger seat and was in the process of closing the door when Carl grabbed the door and stopped him.

"Hey there, you okay?" The sound of his voice registered true concern.

Shocked and surprised by Carl's sudden and unexpected appearance, Dub took a minute to respond. "Yeah, I'm fine. Why do you ask?"

"We haven't seen you all week for mornin' coffee," Carl

shrugged, "and you showed up late tonight and then didn't even say hello."

Dub let what Carl had said sink in before he smiled, "Sorry. I've had a lot on my plate this week. I was out of town for a couple of days taking care of future living arrangements. And then tonight, I guess my brain is a little off."

"That's okay." Carl let go of the truck door. "Kenneth and I were just worried about you. See ya in the mornin'?"

"Plan on it," Dub responded.

"Alright then," Carl took a step back and then before he walked away. "See you then."

Dub pulled the truck door shut, took a small spiral notebook from his pocket, and took a couple of minutes to make himself a note. He looked over at his Bible and tried to remember preacher's message and could not. The bouts of insomnia were beginning to take their toll. He started the truck and prayed he would be able to sleep tonight.

Katherine spent most of Thursday morning prepping the canvas for her next painting. After the last application of gesso had dried, she did a rough outline using the photograph of her and Dub on the tailgate. She wished she had the one his mother had taken of the two of them standing together but since she did not, she improvised. The way his arm hung over her shoulder in the sketch did not look quite right to her. It was something she hoped would fix itself during the process of painting.

She took the picture of the six men peeing off the easel and looked around for a place to set it. Besides the pool table, the game room housed a foosball table and a mahogany shuffleboard. It had not been designed for sitting or for painting. When she realized there was no safe place for the painting, she removed a picture she had bought from the wall and set it in the floor. Using the two screws it had hung on, she hung the canvas in its place, stood back and studied it. Something was still missing.

She returned to the easel and sat the new canvas on it. Tomorrow she would begin, today it was time to decide what she was going to wear for date number five. She tried to pretend she was not excited, but the quickened beat of her heart told a different story.

Her stomach growled and she giggled. The bowl of oatmeal she had for breakfast was not going to hold her until they reached the restaurant. She removed the apron she wore, laid it on the edge of the table, and turned off the light on her way out.

In the kitchen she rummaged through the refrigerator, unable to find anything that sounded good. In the pantry she found a box of granola bars, only one hundred calories each. She took one from the box, started to shut the door, and then decided one might not be enough and grabbed a second bar then returned to the fridge for a bottle of water and headed to her closet.

As she passed her bed, she looked at the clock on the side table. Three hours until date time, plenty of time for a shower.

Dub looked from the picture of his mother to the one of him pushing Katherine on the swing. It was still an hour until he was supposed to pick up Katherine. He stood beside the kitchen table, dressed and ready with nothing to do. He looked at the three boxes at the far end of the table and the thought crossed his mind that he needed to finish going through them. He would do it tomorrow. He took the notebook from his pocket and wrote himself a reminder.

He could feel the first tinge of anxiety pressing against the inside of his chest. Left alone it would start to grow and that he could not allow. He left the kitchen, crossed the living room, and sat down in his recliner. The practice of reading the Bible to ward off apprehension had become his go-to tactic and Psalm 23 was bookmarked for just these kinds of moments.

He read the first verse. "The LORD is my shepherd; I shall not want." He paused, closed his eyes, and said a brief prayer. His eyes opened and he read the second verse. "He maketh me to lie down in green pastures: He leadeth me beside the still waters." Two images superimposed in his mind. The first was of he and Katherine on the tailgate of his dad's old truck. The second was of Katherine standing on the gravel bar with her heels in her hands. In the past, he had simply read. Never had visions appeared.

He read the third verse and began the fourth. "He restoreth my soul: He leadeth me in the paths of righteousness for his name's sake. Yea though I walk through the valley of the shadow of death…" The Humvee was just to his left and slightly behind him. His eyes scanned the buildings ahead. An abandoned vehicle two blocks away caught his eye. Something was not right; he could sense it. The explosion took him off his feet and propelled him twenty feet forward. He landed on his stomach, eyes still on the car. Confused, he tried to figure out why it was still there when in his mind it had been the problem. He tried to roll over, only to find his arm was not working correctly. And then he was being dragged. He did not take his eyes off the rusted old car until Sergeant Frye rolled him over and started screaming at him.

Dub shook the memory from his head and finished reading the passage. He could feel each heartbeat. The valley of death, his valley of death. He read the verse again. This time it did not elicit the nightmare. He wiped sweat from his brow and read the Psalm again. And then again.

Slowly calmness won the battle and the uneasiness retreated. When he was sure it was gone, he closed the Bible and laid it back in its place. He checked his watch. Not enough time for another shower. He removed his shirt on the way to the bathroom. Standing in front of the mirror, he used a washcloth and gave himself a sponge bath from the waist up. *Wash the shit off your face and swab them pits, soldier, you've got a date*, Sergeant Frye in life, and now in death, had always had the most colorful sayings.

A fresh shirt from the closet and Dub checked his watch once more. If he left now, he would be right on time.

CHAPTER 19

Katherine let herself breathe again as Dub pulled to a stop in front of the auto repair shop. A loud ding had sounded just as the indicator light had flashed twice in the gauges on the dashboard. Luck was with them. She had seen the sign just as Dub had begun to slow down.

"Mechanic right there." she pointed. "Hope they're still open."

A tall thin man with a long grey beard and bald head stepped through the open door of the repair shop with a smile. When Dub stepped out of the truck, the man nodded at the tire which was slowly deflating, "Looks like you got here just in time," the mechanic grinned as he spoke.

Katherine had her window down and could hear the hissing as the air escaped the tire. Dub stood for a minute staring at the tire before he spoke. "I hope you're still open for business."

The man chuckled, "Luck is with you, my friend. Normally, I'd already be halfway home by now, but I had a flat myself. Just got it fixed and was about to lock up. Let me grab a jack and I'll see what I can do."

"Thank you," she heard Dub say before walking over to her. "Looks like this might take a minute, do you want to get out?"

"No, I think I'll just sit tight." Katherine looked past him as the mechanic approached, pushing a jack in front of him.

"Sorry about this," Dub apologized.

"You've got nothing to be sorry about." Katherine looked back at him. "It's not like you planned it."

Dub smiled. "No, I can't say I planned it."

Katherine watched in the side mirror as the man removed the tire and rolled it inside. Dub followed along and she reached for her phone. While she waited, she searched and found Ollie's. The picture of the establishment had her wondering if Dub was not trying to pull another fast one on her, but after reading the reviews her mind settled. A quick run through the online menu had her stomach growling and she remembered she had not eaten since noon.

Bored and with nothing else to do, she began to randomly search for whatever came to mind. One search led to another until she found herself reading an article about how to run your own bed and breakfast. She had just finished it when Dub and the mechanic came out with the tire.

Five minutes later, the tire fixed, they pulled out onto the highway and started for Ollie's. At Kingston's one and only stoplight, Dub looked over and grinned. "I don't know about you, but I'm about to starve."

"I was doing okay, until I looked at Ollie's menu online." Katherine tapped the edge of her phone. "Now I'm famished."

As Dub pulled across a set of train tracks, he chuckled. "When I was young, dad used to say, his stomach thought his throat had been slit."

"Mine used to say his belly button was rubbing up against his backbone so hard it was about to rub a hole clean through his skin." Katherine smiled. She was finding it harder and harder to stay angry with Dub. A flashing yellow light ahead warned of an intersection. Katherine looked around at the rural countryside and wondered if the lights were truly necessary.

Dub slowed and turned south. For the next several miles Katherine watched quietly as the countryside flashed by. The sun had started to dip towards the western horizon, causing long shadows across the land. She thought about her own life and wondered how long it would be before her final sunset. Her father had died from a massive heart attack before he reached sixty and her mother had not seen her seventy-fifth birthday. As far as she knew she had no heart problems but even if she used her mother's lifespan, she was looking at maybe twenty more years. Life had seemed so long when she was young and now it seemed so short. Mentally she broke down each of her nearly six decades. Financially she had never wanted, but mentally and emotionally she had had a rough life. Her mother had been fond of saying what does not kill us makes us stronger.

Katherine looked over at Dub. *You're right Momma what doesn't kill us makes us stronger, and I'm not dead yet.*

Dub had no idea what Ollie's looked like until he pulled to a stop in the gravel parking lot. He half expected Katherine to turn red and start cussing before he remembered her saying she had looked it up on her phone. Still the building was not what he had expected. The front porch was wooden, the roof above it half shingle and half metal. The structure was a patchwork of weathered wood and rusted metal siding. An old metal Marlboro sign hung near the front door along with a red and blue neon sign that announced the place was OPEN.

As he escorted Katherine towards the entrance, he noticed an antique icebox and a section of wooden theater seats. He held the door open for Katherine and followed her inside. There did not seem to be an empty table anywhere. The aroma of Creole seasonings filled the air and reminded Dub of his last visit to New Orleans. Music filtered through the conversation from an archway off to his right.

Dub felt like he had been transported to a different time and place. A backwoods swamp around the time of prohibition came to mind. To his left waitresses were coming and going out of what had to be the kitchen. To his right was a fully stocked bar complete with stools. He noticed a deer head with dreadlocks and pearls hanging on the wall and had to smile. The décor was certainly unique and original. A menagerie of tables and chairs spread out in front of him. Katherine pointed past them to a doorway at the end of the bar.

A waitress appeared at his elbow with a plate in each hand. "Welcome to Ollie's, there's a table in the back." She nodded towards the opening Katherine had indicated. "Ya'll find yourself one and someone will be with you shortly."

He placed his hand in the small of Katherine's back and guided her in that direction. At the end of the bar, they passed the restrooms and stepped into a much larger room. In one corner a man strumming a guitar was singing into a microphone. The song was "So You Don't Have To Love Me Anymore", one of Alan Jackson's hits.

The room had a hodge podge of mismatched tables and chairs to choose from, including a line of old booths. A large table that would seat eight and one of the booths were all that was available. Katherine headed for the booth and Dub followed.

The top three-quarters of two of the room's walls had been screened in. As Dub slid into the booth, he prepared himself for the tongue lashing he figured was coming. He looked at Katherine and started to speak but found her staring at something over his shoulder. When he turned a waitress had walked up and was asking them for their drink orders.

"Sweet tea for me," Katherine raised her voice above the volume of the music, "and if you have a drink menu, I'd like to see it."

"Just sweet tea for me," Dub told the young woman who turned and made her way back across the room.

"I love this place." Katherine was swaying in her seat to the music. "It's so... I don't even know how to put it... different, but in a good way."

Dub let out a sigh of relief. "I'm glad you like it. Carl was not exactly forthcoming when it came to the looks of this place. He only told me the food was excellent."

"Well, I love it," Katherine repeated. "Oh my, look at that."

she pointed out the trunk of a tree beside a table in the middle of the room. "How cool is that?"

Dub turned in his seat to look and realized the tree had not grown through the roof but rather the room had been built around the tree. While he was still studying the tree, the song finished, and the singer announced the band would be taking a short break. He stepped back from the mic and the click of a sound system turning on could be heard, followed by Randy Travis's voice singing "Hard Rock Bottom of Your Heart".

As Randy sang about letting a true love down and asking for forgiveness, Dub wished he could go back in time and do things differently. He was not sure if it was the lyrics or if Katherine could read his mind, but for whatever reason, she reached across the table and took his hands in hers. "You're still a jackass, but I forgive you."

"For Dairy Queen, or the dam, or not tellin' you about goin' to church?" He gave her hand a little squeeze.

"You really are clueless." Katherine shook her head and squeezed back. "I forgive you for leaving me and breaking my heart."

"Oh." He knew he should say something more, but the lump in his throat would not let words pass. He smiled and tried to swallow the emotions. *Not so tough now, marine*, Sergeant Frye's voice took over.

"And just so you know, you're still not off the hook for the church thing." She gently squeezed once more and then released his hands.

Katherine could not remember the last time she had eaten so much food. She could have made a whole meal on the gator balls they had for an appetizer. The Catfish Suzie Mae meal she ordered had two large catfish fillets smothered in the most wonderful sauce she had ever tasted and was served on a bed of rice. It came with one side, and she had asked for a salad. Dub had insisted on desert. He ordered a slice of homemade buttermilk pie. The deep-fried Twinkie on the menu caught her eye. It was served with a choice of sauces, and although she was not sure where she was going to put it, the thought *you only live once* popped into her head, and she told the waitress she would take it with the chocolate sauce.

The band had returned from their break shortly after their food had arrived and she had enjoyed listening to the music they played while eating. As soon as the waitress left with their dessert order, Dub stood up, and offered her his hand. "Would you care to dance, my lady?"

Halfway through her second margarita, she smiled and took his hand. He helped her to her feet and the two navigated through the tables full of other customers to the small area where they had seen other couples dancing earlier. The floor was theirs alone for the moment. Dub pulled her into his arms as the band began a new song. Slowly he moved along in a close two-step as the instrumental intro played. Katherine did not recognize the song until the singer stepped up to the microphone and began to sing Rascal Flatts' "Bless the Broken Road."

She had never really listened to the words before, and as Dub moved her around in a tight circle, the lyrics found their way into her heart, and she laid her head on his shoulder. Later she would blame the tears on the margaritas.

The song ended and he led her back to their booth. She found a napkin and dabbed at her eyes. "I'm sorry. I don't know what's gotten into me."

Dub reached across the table and took her hand. "Kat, I should be the one apologizing. I should never have left. I have been running all my life and now the best years of my life are behind me. And I wish I had them back so I could give every one of them to you."

"Dammit, Dub." The tears started again. "You promised you were not going to try to win my heart."

He smiled, but she could see the pain behind it. "I'm not trying to win your heart, Kat. I wish I was... I wish I could, but I think it's too late for that."

"It's never too late." Katherine heard her voice but felt like it was someone else speaking.

"Kat," Dub pulled her hand across the table and kissed the top of it, "if you don't remember anything else from this night, I want you to remember what you just said."

"It's never too late?" She managed between sniffles and swallowed hard.

"Yes, Kat." Dub laid her hand back on the table. "It's never too late."

CHAPTER 20

At the door to her house, Katherine surprised Dub by asking, "Would you like to come in for a minute?"

Oh, you've done it now, you sly dog, Sergeant Frye chuckled in his head. *I hope your little marine is up to the task.*

He mentally shook the sergeant from his mind, and stammered, "Kat it's nearly midnight."

Katherine chuckled. "My goodness, Dub Taylor, you look like you've seen a ghost. Relax, I'm not trying to seduce you. I just have something I want to show you. It won't take but a minute."

Stand down, marine, Sergeant Frye's voice returned. *The mission has been aborted. Repeat, the mission is a no go.*

Dub cussed the sergeant under his breath as he followed Katherine into the house. From the exterior, the place had looked massive, but now as he followed her in he found himself speculating about how big it really was and questioning why she needed a home so big. The entry way was nearly as big as his living room. He looked up over the balcony railing and found himself wondering if his house had as much square footage as what was upstairs. Somehow, he doubted it.

"You have a beautiful home." Dub looked into what he figured was the living room.

"I don't know that I would call it a home." Katherine pointed to an opening beside the staircase leading up. "It's just a very big house."

Katherine did not bother giving him the grand tour. She led him through what he figured was a formal dining room, the kitchen, a den, and into a game room. The first thing he noticed was the tarp thrown over a table in the center of the room and the mess on top of it. It took a second before it registered that there was most likely a pool table under the nylon cover. On top of it was an easel with a rough sketch. Katherine attempted to direct his attention to the wall beside the table, but he could not take his eyes off the canvas in front of him.

"My arm is wrong." He pointed at it.

Katherine turned to look. "I'm hoping it corrects itself when I paint it. The pictures you gave me… well, let's just say I had to adapt them."

Dub looked from the drawing to her. "You paint?"

"Yes, Dub, I paint." She pointed to the wall. "This is what I wanted to show you."

He stepped around the edge of the pool table and stopped. His eyes widened and his mouth dropped. There he was, third from the left, peeing into the darkness. Every detail jumped off the canvas at him. The stitching on the pockets of his Wranglers. The sweat stains around the band of his old Stetson hat. But most of all the amber stream between his legs.

"Good gosh, woman," his voice cracked. "Why in the world did you paint that?"

"Because I wanted to," Katherine laughed. "Pretty damn good, isn't it?"

Dub stepped closer and studied it for a minute. "It's amazing, actually. You even managed to get the lighting perfect. But what's with all the cowboy hats."

"What do you mean?" Katherine stepped up beside him.

"Well that's Carl, and there's Jim." He pointed out the guys to his left in the picture. "And neither of them wear hats." He continued down the line of men. "That's me, and then Pete, John, and Kenneth. Besides me, only Kenneth had on a western hat that night."

"Artistic license," Katherine turned her head as she spoke.

Dub looked at her. "What is artistic license?"

131

"It means that as the painter, as the artist, I have the freedom to change the scene to my liking," Katherine bobbled her head from side to side as she spoke.

Dub laughed. "Well, I think Carl would appreciate you covering up his bald head, but I'm not so sure any of the guys will be thrilled about the way you have them posed."

"Don't want to be painted taking a whiz, don't piss in view of a bunch of old ladies." Katherine turned back to the canvas. "But I didn't bring you in here to discuss the subject matter. There's something missing. I can't figure it out, and it's bothering me."

Dub studied the painting for another long second, "It looks perfect to me. Only thing left as far as I'm concerned is the signature."

"Holy hell, Dub, that's it!" Katherine gave him a quick peck on the cheek. "I forgot to sign it."

Shocked, Dub took a step back. Katherine laughed. "Damn, Dub, you've gone all red again. I told you I wasn't going to seduce you. It was just a little thank you kiss, now go on, it's late." She pointed back the way they had come. "Time for you to go, so this old lady can get ready for bed."

Mason shook his head as Katherine and Dub sat across the desk in their usual seats, discussing possible activities for their sixth date. Dealing with the two of them was like riding a rollercoaster backwards, blindfolded, through a carwash. Even though one knew what to expect, they never knew when it was going to hit.

"I'd love to go dancing," Katherine was saying.

"I'll see what I can figure out." Dub turned to Mason as he spoke.

It took Mason a moment to figure out Dub was looking to him for advice. He was not a dancer. He had never been very coordinated and the few times he had attempted it, he had walked away feeling foolish. .

"Can't help you there," he shrugged. "I don't dance."

"That's okay." Dub nodded, "Put us down for next Friday." He turned to Katherine. "Say five o'clock?"

"That works for me." Katherine nodded.

Mason took out his planner. "A week from today, five o'clock." He spoke aloud as he wrote their names on the schedule. "I don't work on weekends, so I guess we'll meet here the Monday following the date. One o'clock seems to be our usual time. Does that work for the two of you?"

He received affirmation from them both before entering the appointment. "I guess that will about do it for today then." He closed the book and looked up at them. "I'll see you in ten days."

"Sounds good to me." Katherine smiled at him. Mason was not sure how to respond. The smile was genuine, almost friendly. He could not help but think of his visits with the Lord. It was not a miracle he decided. Close to, but not quite one.

When she rose and stuck her hand out, he almost let his jaw drop open, but caught it at the last instant. Still wary, he stood and shook her hand. The image of a hole opening beneath his feet and a demon's hand pulling him into it flashed across his mind. He felt rather foolish when she released his hand and turned to Dub. "Call me when you decide where we're going, so I can figure out an outfit."

"I will." Dub stood and escorted her across the room. He pulled an envelope from his pocket and placed it in her hand. "I have some additional business with Mr. Boyd," he said as he opened the door for her. "I'll be in touch."

For a split second, Mason expected the two to share a kiss before she left. Why the idea popped into his head, he was not sure, but as soon as it did, he chuckled, then covered it with a cough as Dub turned back.

"We need to talk about the seventh date." Dub said as he

walked back to his seat. "Do you have time now, or should I make an appointment for some time next week?"

Katherine tossed her keys on the table next to the garage door on her way into the house. In the kitchen she dropped her purse onto one of the bar chairs, laid the envelope Dub had given her on the countertop, and began to gather the makings of a sandwich. After the meal at Ollie's the previous night, she had been certain she would not need to eat again for a solid week. The rumbling of her stomach told her she had been wrong.

When she had the sandwich made, she sat down with it and a glass of sweet tea and began to eat. The envelope caught her eye, and in between bites she opened it. She eased the contents out and found herself looking at the picture she had wanted for the painting she was working on, the image of her and Dub standing on the back of truck. Her artistic eye studied the arm draped over her shoulder and she knew how to fix it in her sketch.

Her eyes moved from his hands to the face of the young girl in the picture. There was a sparkle in her eyes, a smile on her face, and an aura of hope and love in the way she held herself. Katherine felt the tears begin to well up. She laid the sandwich aside and let them come. There before her was the spirit she had lost. The person she was meant to be.

She looked at the young man standing beside her. He looked confused and a bit embarrassed, but happy. A perfect picture of what should have been. It was not until she started to set the photograph down that she realized there was another behind it.

The second photo was one of Dub swinging her on the old rope swing behind his house. The tears flowed harder. She laid the two pictures beside each other on the countertop and cried. She let the frustration of the past flow down her cheeks and onto the marble bar. She made no attempt to stop it. She did not try to control it. It came in waves. Just when she thought she was done, another wave would begin.

Somehow as they flowed, the tears turned from those of frustration to tears of determination and then to hope. She would find that spirit. She would become who she was meant to be even if she died trying.

The tears stopped flowing and she used a napkin to wipe her eyes. She put the photographs back into the envelope and finished her sandwich. Once she had straightened up the kitchen and returned all the sandwich makings to their places, she took the envelope with the photographs into the game room. She set the one of her and Dub on the tailgate in front of the sketch on the easel and backed up to look at them together. For a second, she contemplated fixing the arm then decided it would have to wait until after she had taken a nap. Exhaustion was making it hard for her to keep her eyes open.

She took the second picture with her through the house and into her bathroom. In the mirror, she noticed her reflection. Her makeup was a mess. Mascara had stained half circles under each of her eyes and left black streaks down her cheeks through her base, leaving the skin beneath bare. She laid the photograph aside and washed the remaining makeup off in the sink.

When she was finished, she changed into loose fitting silk pants, an oversized t-shirt, and a pair of bright pink fluffy socks. She took the picture into her room, and laid it beside the Bible on her nightstand, then set the timer on her cellphone for one hour, crawled into bed, and drifted off to the image of Dub waltzing her around a dance floor.

Mason stared down at the notes he had taken. At the top of a yellow legal pad, he had written in big block letters — THE SEVENTH DATE. As was his habit, he had skipped every other line and bulleted each new topic with a large asterisk on the left side of the paper. He reviewed the notes on the first page and flipped it to the back. By the bottom of the second page, his heart felt like a ten-ton stone in his chest. Halfway through the third, he had begun to once again question God and whether or not miracles existed.

Without finishing the third page, he laid the notepad down, made his way to the file cabinet, and poured himself a drink. *This world is cruel and life ain't fair,* he heard his father's voice as he downed the first drink and poured himself another. Before he began to drink it, he held it up in a toast, "You got that right, dad."

CHAPTER 21

Three boxes were left, labeled—76 & 77, 78 & 79, and 80 with a long dash after it. Color images of his life from age twelve to sixteen, maybe seventeen. He had spent the weekend avoiding the task of looking through them. Saturday, he had checked the entire barn and all the outbuildings, knowing before he began that there was nothing in them he would want to take with him. Sunday, he had gone through each room of the house except for Ben's room. He had been unable to open the door to it since returning home after his mother's death.

He had spent his life constantly on the move up until he retired from the military. His lifestyle had not allowed for an accumulation of material things. If he could not fit it into a duffle and a carry on, he did not need it. The small stack of pictures on the table, his clothes, and an old quilt his mother had made him were all he planned to take out of the house.

Now it was Monday afternoon and he had run out of ways to stall. He seated himself in his usual chair and opened the next box of photographs, his seventh and eighth grade years. The boy in the pictures had begun to fill out a bit. In the back half of the box, the image of Ben showed a tall muscular kid with a grin that spoke of trouble. Many of the photos of Ben included Vickie, who seldom smiled because of the braces she wore.

Any picture he found in the box that had Katherine or Vickie he dropped into a pile. Katherine, who had been a year behind him in school was still a short skinny little girl in all of the photos in the first box, but towards the back of the second box, she had started to blossom. In the last package of pictures in the box, he found a photo of Katherine leaned back against one of the poles in the barn. He was sitting on the corral railing beside her, and he and Katherine were looking at each other. He had spent the day throwing bales of hay up to Ben who was stacking them in the loft. The curve of her hips and breast were clearly visible. He was shirtless and his skin glistened with sweat. He remembered the conversation his mother had interrupted with the picture.

"I think I want us to be more than friends." He had finally gotten up the courage to say it.

Katherine had looked up at him and smiled. "What took you so long?"

He had looked away, not sure of himself. "I guess I was afraid it might not work out and I'd lose my best friend."

"So, I'm your best friend." She had giggled.

"You know you are." Dub had looked back down at her, forcing himself to look into her eyes even though he was blushing. "And I don't want to do anything to mess that up."

"Me either." Katherine reached out and slapped his leg. "I was just teasin' you."

The two had smiled and his mother had snapped the photograph. He never knew if his mother had heard the conversation or not. If she had, she never let on.

That had been the summer before the accident. He and Katherine had spent a lot of time talking about going steady. It had been an awkward time of long walks, of holding hands, and waiting for the right time to kiss her.

After staring at the photograph for a long time, he decided Katherine should have it, and added it to her pile. He put the rest of the prints from the pack back into the envelope and placed it in the back of the box before snugging the lid in its place. Seven down, one to go. He pulled the last box across the table and took a deep breath.

Opening it, inside he found his mother's camera in the middle of the box wedged between two stacks of envelopes.

Those in the front were the kind photographs normally come in, those in the back were plain white letter-size envelopes. He slowly worked his way through the front stack.

Pictures of Ben in his letterman's jacket. Some of Vickie in the same jacket worn over her cheerleading uniform with Ben's arm around her. Another set of Ben taken around the barn. Dub remembered the day they were taken. Senior pictures his mother had made Ben take, telling him he would appreciate them later in life. The last envelope had images from the homecoming football game. Ben and some of his senior friends posed against the field house. One of Ben and Dub together both looking very serious. The next one taken right after when they had lost it, and both begun to laugh. The last one in the package was the last image of Ben alive.

It had been taken at the end of the game. He and Ben still in pads with their arms around each other's shoulders with Vickie beside Ben and Katherine next to Dub, and each brother had their other arm around their girl. The final score on the board behind them was twenty to twenty-one. Dub had managed to round the edge and get a hand on the ball causing the extra point to go wide.

He had often wondered if the game had gone into overtime if it would have thrown the timing of the accident off. It was the reason he never played football again and could not bring himself to return to school. He had finished his studies at home and enlisted in the Marine Corps as soon as he turned eighteen. If it had not been for his mother's refusal to sign for him, he would have left even earlier. He knew she had hoped he would change his mind right up until the day he left.

He laid the photograph on Katherine's pile. Somehow that did not seem right, he picked it back up and put it back into the envelope it had been in before placing it back in the box. *Mission accomplished, soldier*, Sergeant Frye's congratulations did little to lift his mood. He took the envelopes from the back of the box and spread them out on the table. There were seven in all.

With a deep sigh, he decided they would have to wait.

Jenn propped herself against the foosball table. It was Tuesday evening and Katherine was hard at work painting. She had most of the background in and was about to begin work on the truck.

"So, Friday night." Jenn watched her mother working. "I guess that's the next big date?"

Katherine turned around. "Damn Jenn, do you have Mason's office bugged?"

Jenn laughed. "No, why do you ask?"

"Well, I haven't told anyone when the date is." Katherine pointed the paintbrush at her daughter. "And Mason can't. That would be against attorney-client privilege or some such shit. And I have a problem thinking Dub would run his mouth, so how the hell do you know the date is this Friday?"

"Simple deduction." Jenn smiled. "Date number one was on a Sunday, each date after that moved up one day in the week. Last week's date, number five, was on Thursday that means the next one must be on Friday and..."

"The seventh date will be on a Saturday." Katherine finished the sentence.

"Exactly." Jenn raised her hands and, in her mind, said *TADA*!

"Well, I'll be damned." Katherine turned back to her canvas. "I wonder why I did not see it?"

"Maybe, because you've been too busy falling for Mr. Taylor." Jenn pushed herself away from the foosball table and moved to the other side of the pool table so she could see her mother's face.

"I am not falling for Mr. Taylor." Katherine pointed the brush at her again. "I enjoyed our last date and I'm looking forward to our next one, but I am not falling for Dub."

"Well, that attitude is a far cry from your first couple of dates." Jenn grinned. "I'm wondering if there's a chance *someone* might get lucky this Friday."

"Jennifer Lynn," Katherine scolded, then added more softly, "that ain't damn likely."

"Not even if he plays his cards right?" Jenn continued to rib her mother.

"Child, there ain't enough cards in a deck for that to happen." Her mother responded in an exaggerated Okie accent and added a little head bobble with it.

Jenn was enjoying the banter. "I guess you never played poker with the jokers as wild cards, huh?"

"I don't know what the hell you're talking about." Katherine drew her eyebrows down. "And when have you ever played poker?"

"Now, Momma," Jenn giggled, "I cain't tell you all my secrets. That just wouldn't be lady like." Jenn wiggled her eyebrows. "But if you two do end up in a game of strip poker, you make him take out the wild cards before you start. And that's all I'm gonna say."

"Strip poker, have you lost your mind?" Katherine shook her head, then as she turned back to her painting. "You are a rotten child, yes you are."

Katherine arrived at the church five minutes before services were due to start Wednesday night. She had gotten lost in the painting and lost track of time. Bible in one hand, keys in the other, she hustled across the parking lot and into the building only to find Dub standing just inside the door visiting with Brother Jerry.

Both men had turned when she entered and now she stood trying to think of something to say. She opened her mouth and then closed it again. Dub smiled and instinctively she smiled back. Brother Jerry said hello, excused himself, and started down the center aisle towards the pulpit.

"Would you like to sit with me?" Dub motioned to the back pew as he spoke.

"I would love to." Katherine found her voice and followed him to the far end and sat down beside him.

She found comfort in the feeling of him sitting so close. It was a strange sensation. She tried to remember if she had ever felt it before and her mind took her back to the tailgate of a pickup. She shook her head. It seemed as if everything in her life hinged on that homecoming night so long ago.

Jenn's question about where Dub attended church popped into her head. She turned to look at him and caught him staring at her. She blushed and in a hushed whisper spoke, "Do you attend service here regularly?"

Brother Jerry chose that instant to step to the pulpit and ask everyone to bow their heads. When the prayer ended, Dub leaned over. "My church attendance is a bit complicated, but if you'll ask me again later, I'll explain it to you."

CHAPTER 22

"Are you in a hurry to get home?" Katherine stood beside her car with her Bible and her keys.

Dub, who had walked with her out of the church, thought before he spoke, "This isn't some trick is it?"

Katherine gave him a confused look.

"You wouldn't be tryin' to slip an extra date in on me, so you could get the land earlier, would you?" He rephrased the question doing his best to look stern.

"Dub Taylor, you are such an..." she stopped and looked back towards the church.

"An ass." Dub finished without turning to look at the church. "But that still does not answer the question."

"No, Dub." Katherine rolled her eyes. "I'm not asking you out on a date. I just thought we could have a visit and you could tell me about your church attendance." She held up her right hand. "I swear this visit will not be construed in any way as one of the seven dates."

"Alright, then let's go get some ice cream." He grinned and opened her car door for her.

Dairy Queen was crowded with the after-church crowd, but their booth was open, and Katherine made her way to it quickly. She slid into the bench on the backside so she could watch Dub who stood in line at the counter waiting to order. The young man behind the register handed a man in jeans and a brown sport coat his receipt. The man stepped away from the counter, turned and began to look for his party. Everyone in line moved forward. Dub moved up, then turned and caught Katherine watching him. With a half grin, he winked before turning back around.

A young woman in the booth adjacent to Katherine's giggled. Katherine turned at the sound and the woman smiled at her and nodded. Katherine felt her face flush and smiled back. The young woman sat alone. An empty tray pushed back away from her was littered with the wrapper from a hamburger and a basket that Katherine guessed probably held French fries at one point. On the table in front of her was a textbook and a writing tablet. Katherine wondered whether she was a high school student or if she was attending Murray State, the junior college at the edge of town.

"What are you studying?" Katherine spoke just loud enough for her to hear above the buzz of conversation and kitchen noise.

The young woman raised the front half of the book she was working out of so that Katherine could see the front cover. "Tonight it's chemistry."

"High school or college?" Katherine watched as she lowered the book back to the table.

"College," she replied, "but thank you. It's been a while since anyone mistook me for a high school student."

Katherine pursed her lips. "I find that hard to believe. You can't be that old. Oh, by the way, I'm Katherine."

"Nice to meet you, Katherine. I'm Judi." The woman smiled. "And I'll be thirty-one next week."

Katherine tried not to look astonished, but she knew she was failing from the look on Judi's face. "I would never have guessed. You look so young. But then what do I know, I'm just an old woman whose been out of touch for way too long."

"You are not an old woman." Judi cocked her head to the side. "And I'm not buying that out of touch stuff at all. I saw the way your husband winked at you."

"Oh, my," Katherine shook her head, "He's not my husband. He's just a friend. And I am old. I have a daughter who's only a couple of years older than you."

"Now I find that hard to buy." Judi straightened her head but turned it and looked sideways at Katherine.

"That I have a daughter your age?" Katherine smiled. She was enjoying the visit and Judi's compliments made her feel good if not young.

"That," Judi nodded towards the counter where Dub had made it to the front of the line, "and I find it hard to believe you and that man are just friends. I saw the way he looked at you and until you started talking to me, you couldn't keep your eyes off him."

Katherine could feel the rush of blood to her cheeks and knew she was blushing again. "I think you have the wrong idea." Judi raised her eyebrows in question and Katherine began to wonder if she was lying to herself.

"One vanilla dip cone for the lady." Katherine turned at Dub's voice to see him holding out the chocolate coated ice cream.

"Oh, thank you." She took it as he eased into the seat across from her. "This is Judi." She introduced her new friend. "She is studying out at the college, but we hadn't gotten around to discussing her major."

Dub raised the Stetson from his head. "It's very nice to meet you." He smiled then settled it back into place.

"Likewise, sir." Judi smiled and nodded. "And I'm working on a nursing degree."

The conversation quickly turned to Judi's studies and the courses required for her to meet her goals. Katherine had finished her ice cream cone before it occurred to her that she and Dub had yet to discuss his church attendance.

"I don't mean to get too personal," Katherine looked from Dub to Judi, "but do you attend church?"

"I used to," Judi admitted with a frown. "But it's been quite a while ago."

Katherine asked her for a piece of paper and borrowed the pencil she had been taking notes with. "You are officially invited to the All Faith Christian Church as my guest." She wrote the name of the church and her name on the paper and handed it and the pencil back to Judi.

"That is so sweet." Judi placed a hand over her heart. "I will definitely try to attend."

When Katherine looked at Dub, a smile had spread across his face and he seemed to be glowing. It caught her off guard and she blushed.

Judi gathered her study materials, stood, and started to pick up her tray.

"If you will leave that," Dub stopped her, "I'll be glad to take it on our way out."

"Thank you so much." Judi turned. "It was so nice to meet y'all."

Dub nodded. Katherine reached out and touched Judi's arm. "It was nice to meet you, too. I hope we didn't keep you from getting your studying done."

"Not at all." Judi leaned down. "I really just need some time away from my housemates. Thank you for a lovely visit."

As she walked away, Dub reached across the table and took Katherine's hand in his and gave it a squeeze. "It's nice to have the old Kat back."

Katherine squeezed back before pulling her hand away. "That will be enough of that. Now let's talk about you and church."

Dub reached over and took the tray from Judi's table and placed it between he and Katherine. He moved the empty fry basket to one corner of the tray, took the empty hamburger wrapper and set it in the far corner. The papers from around his and Katherine's cones were lying on the table, and he used them

146

to fill the last two corners. A couple of napkins were left from the handful he had brought with him to the booth. One of these he wadded up and tossed up on the tray as well.

"I don't know exactly how many churches the town of Tishomingo has." Dub took a small blue spiral notebook from his pocket as he spoke. "But in the six months I have been back I have been attending five of them."

He watched Katherine as he flipped open the notebook. "Tonight, as you know, I was at the All Faith Christian Church." He laid the little tablet on the table and made a mark through the entry for the church, then turned it around so Katherine could see the page.

On the line below the one he had just marked through were the words — Baptist Church, the line below that held but one word — Pentecostal. The lines on the bottom half of the page were blank.

"When I first got to town," Dub explained as he returned the notebook to his shirt pocket, "I met Carl one mornin' at the coffee shop. He was sittin' by himself and invited me to join him. While we were visiting, he invited me to the Methodist church where he attends services. That afternoon, I went to get my hair trimmed, and Pete, you remember Pete, he's my barber. Well, he invited me to his church, the Church of Christ. Then when I went to the feed store to see if mom had any outstanding debts there Jim Lovett invited me to the Baptist Church... and well, you get the idea."

Katherine nodded. "Yes, but that does not explain why you attend five different churches and how you decide which to attend on any given Sunday, and Wednesday, I guess."

"You're right." Dub held up a finger and smiled. "And at first, I had a hard time deciding what I should do." He pointed at the tray, "And then John asked me to come to the Pentecostal Church and if you haven't figured it out yet, Kenneth insisted I visit the church we just came from, and all of this happened in a two week period."

147

"So, you just started going to all of them?" Dub could tell by her tone of voice she was questioning his sanity.

"Kind of, but not really." He touched the tip of his finger to his temple, "I never claimed to be all that up here and as far as spiritual things are concerned, I guess you could say I feel kind of like Moses when God told him to go lead the Israelites out of Egypt."

"Tishomingo isn't Egypt and I'm pretty sure choosing a church to attend is not as big as the task the Lord asked of Moses." Katherine held up a finger as soon as she finished the sentence. "However, now that I think about it, when I first told Jenn I was moving back here she referred to this as B.F.E. and when I asked her what that meant she said Bum F. Egypt, only she said the whole word."

"Yes, I'm familiar with abbreviation." Dub chuckled. "And choosing a church might not seem that big of a deal, but I have learned that it doesn't matter how big or small the task is, it always works out better if the Lord is in control."

Katherine put a finger on the edge of the tray. "The Lord told you to go to all these churches? Did He also tell you which one to attend on which days?"

"When you put it that way it does sound rather odd." Dub smiled. "I was praying about which church to attend one night, and it came to me that if I had a system, I could attend them all and not hurt anyone's feelings."

"A system?" Katherine tapped her finger on the tray.

"Yes, a system," Dub pointed at the pieces of trash scattered around. "Carl asked me first." He pointed at the fry basket. "So the first one I attended was the Methodist church. That was on a Sunday. On Wednesday night, I went to the Church of Christ since Pete asked me second, and then on the next Sunday to the Baptist church with Jim." Each time he mentioned a church he pointed to another item on the tray.

Katherine had been following along with her finger. Dub had not yet pointed at the hamburger wrapper or the wadded-up napkin. When he looked up, she was staring at him, eyes narrowed. "I have two questions."

"Okay, shoot."

"First, what do you do when you've crossed out all the churches in your little blue book, if no one has invited you to their church again?" She pointed around the tray.

"I stay home and read my Bible." Dub moved what was left of the stack of napkins up next to the tray and tapped on it with his finger. "Next question."

A smile spread across Katherine's face. She looked him dead in the eye and pointed at the hamburger wrapper. "Is this the All Faith Christian Church or the Pentecostal?" And she began to laugh.

Dub shook his head. "Whichever you want it to be." He began to laugh with her.

"You do realize none of the preachers or pastors or members of the congregation would much care for you using trash to represent their churches?" Katherine managed through the laughter.

"Lord have mercy." Dub pushed everything to the middle of the tray and looked around.

His action caused Katherine to laugh even harder. *She does have a point*, Sergeant Frye chose to put his two cents in. *You think combat was hard, soldier, you just let one of them Methodists find out you said their church resembled an empty french fry basket.*

Dub shook his head and started to rise. Katherine reached out before he could and grabbed his hand and pulled him back into his seat. "Just a second. One more question." She held up a finger as she continued to laugh.

Dub was not sure if the finger indicated the one question, or if she was asking for a second to get herself under control. He understood the humor in what she had said but did not find it nearly as funny.

"Serious question." She stopped laughing and dropped the finger. "Did God tell you to take me to Brother Jerry's church?"

Dub smiled. "No, Kat. Brother Jerry told me to invite you to church when I told him you had taught a Sunday school class before, so I decided to use one of our dates. That way you would have to go."

"I believe that might fall under spiritual manipulation," Katherine pointed at him, "and I'm not sure that's legal."

Dub chuckled. "You're going to church. You're plannin' on teachin' a class. I don't know if I'd say it was manipulation. I think it might be best to simply file it under the old sayin'— God works in mysterious way."

CHAPTER 23

Katherine spent Thursday morning putting the final touches on her second painting. The photograph Dub had given her lay on the table beside the easel. It had helped greatly, and she had no doubt that without it she would have struggled getting Dub's arm correctly positioned.

At noon she made herself a bite of lunch before cleaning up and driving herself into town. She had arrived at the Hair Raisin' Salon & Nail Parlor twenty minutes before her appointed time. Jenn had agreed to cut and style her hair and while she was excited about it, she was also apprehensive. It had been a long while since she had done anything at all with her hair and she was not sure exactly what she wanted.

Jenn was just finishing up a perm and Lori, Jenn's coworker and half owner of the salon, was waiting on her next appointment when Katherine walked through the door. Lori found a couple of magazines for her to look through while she waited, and she sat turning pages and listening to the chitchat between the other three women in the room.

"Finding anything you like?" Jenn asked as she continued to work with her customer's hair.

"Not really." Katherine flipped another page. "I think maybe just a trim. Get the dead ends off and straighten it up a little. I don't think I want anything drastic."

"You know what I think?" Jenn stopped what she was doing and looked at her mother.

Katherine looked up from her magazine. "What do you think?"

Jenn's eyes sparkled, and she smiled. "I think we should call Mr. Taylor and ask him what he likes."

Bright red, Katherine glared at her daughter. "Jennifer Lynn, you know what I think?"

"Yea, yea," Jenn laughed as she replied, "I know what you think. I need a whoopin'."

"Yes, yes you do." Lori came to Katherine's defense. "You should be ashamed of yourself."

"Well, I'm not." Jenn continued to laugh.

"So, what do you plan to do with Mr. Taylor's place once he's gone?" Lori turned her back on Jenn as she spoke.

Katherine's brain stopped. The magazine in front of her forgotten, she looked up at Lori and her mind froze. If someone had reached into her chest and pulled out her heart it would not have phased her. As a matter of fact, in her mind it would have explained the instant empty hole she felt where her heart should have been. Why had it not occurred to her that Dub would leave? It was not just the acreage she had been leasing she was going to obtain when the seventh date was over. It was also the twenty acres his house sat on. He would be homeless. Where would he go? How could he go?

It took all the willpower she possessed not to rush out the door and drive straight to his house. One of the magazines fell from her lap onto the floor.

"Mrs. Williams, are you okay?" Lori stepped over to her and retrieved the magazine.

"Where will he go?" Katherine was not speaking to Lori, but to herself.

Lori stood with the magazine in hand. "I don't know, ma'am."

Dub walked down the hall and opened the door to what was to become his new home. It was not fancy. It was not spacious.

Neither of those had been on his list of requirements when he had begun his search for a place to live. Location had not been a top priority either. When he had found this place, he had known almost immediately it was what he was looking for and in just a few days it would be his.

He had made the trip from Tishomingo to Sulphur with no problems. The navigational software on his phone was a blessing. He would not officially move in until Monday, but he had gotten it okayed so that he could move his few possessions in early.

He did not bother to unpack but dropped his military issue duffle in the closet and placed the envelope with the pictures he had decided to keep on the shelf above the clothes rod. The quilt his mother had made him was folded and he laid it on top of the duffle. He pulled his notebook from his pocket and checked it. Back to Tish was the next thing on his list. He put the notebook back in its place and made his way back to the door. At the door he turned and took one more look. It was enough. It would be a good home.

Back in his truck, he plugged the phone in and tapped the navigation icon. After a few seconds, he typed in Tishomingo and waited. It gave him two options. He chose the shortest and laid the phone on the console. Siri's voice came through the speakers and instructed him to turn right onto Fairlane Avenue.

Tomorrow was his date with Katherine. He smiled at the thought, pulled out of the parking area, and turned right.

The argument within Katherine's mind and heart continued. She sat on the settee in front of her vanity and stared at her reflection. In the short time that she had been back in contact with Dub Taylor, something had happened to her. She had changed. There was no doubt about that because the way she felt about the world, about herself, about just about everything was different now. Even the way she felt about Dub himself was different and that was where the argument had reached an impasse. Her heart said it was love, her head begged to differ.

"He's a jackass," she told the woman in the mirror, "an old friend at best."

An old friend my ass, the lips of the woman in the mirror did not move, but in Katherine's head her words rang clear and true. *You're in love with him.*

"I am most certainly not," Katherine argued.

Then what was that whole Where-will-he-go shit back at the salon?

Katherine glared into the mirror. "I can be concerned for a friend. That does not mean I'm in love with him."

You just keep telling yourself that, and maybe one day you will actually believe it.

"Oh, piss off!" Katherine rolled her eyes and picked up a hairbrush.

Even without looking, she knew the reflection was laughing at her.

Dub swung the door to Ben's room open and looked inside but did not enter. On his trip back from Sulphur, he had not been able to quiet the voice in his head that said he needed to see the room one last time. Now he stood and wondered why? Why, in the forty years since the accident, had nothing in the room been changed? Everything was exactly as Ben had left it that day. The Dallas comforter on the bed and the poster of Roger Staubach above it reminded Dub of his brother's love for football and his Cowboys, and the way he would constantly tell anyone who would listen that one day he was going to lead them back to the super bowl.

In less than the time it took to blink, that dream had disappeared and along with it his parents' happiness. The loss of their oldest child had devastated them. Dub had watched both his mother and father shut down. He wondered if that had not played a part in his own unwillingness to have children.

An old memory formed in the back of his mind and began to work its way forward. His first instinct was to shut the door and block it out. Instead, he stepped into the doorway and leaned against the doorframe just as had he had done those many years ago.

"What are you hollering for?" his sixteen-year-old self looked down at the memory of his brother sitting on the bed shoving thigh pads into his football pants.

Ben had looked up. "I want to ask you a question."

"So, ask it." Dub remembered thinking he was going to ask him if they were riding together to the game or if he was going to take his own truck.

"Did you vote for Vickie for homecoming queen?" Ben's voice had held a note of aggravation.

Vickie had upset Katherine the day of the vote, and Dub was not sure that even had she not done that he would have voted for her. "What does it matter? She's gonna win anyway. We both know that."

"It matters to me." Ben's backed up the words with a stern look. "She's my girl."

"Who I vote for is my decision." Dub had turned to leave.

"And who I choose to throw the ball to is my decision." Ben had hollered up the hall at him. "You remember that tonight at the game, little brother."

Dub pushed himself off the doorframe, let the memory fade, and shut the door. He and Ben had seldom seen eye-to-eye, but they would have killed for each other. That conversation and the fact that Ben had not thrown a single pass his way during the game were among the reasons he had refused to leave the party with Ben.

So many little choices a person makes in their lifetime. How different would one's life be if they had chosen differently just one time? What if he had ignored Ben that night? What if he had simply walked up the hall and left in his own truck? What if Ben had thrown him the ball at least once during the game? What if he had ridden home with his parents and taken his own truck instead of riding with Ben to the party? And of course, the question that had plagued him forever: what if he and Katherine had left with Ben and Vickie?

And the answer — then there would not have been room for Tim and his girlfriend. Ben would not have driven to Caddo and so would not have stopped to relieve himself. Ben would be alive. He would have married Vickie, Dub would have married Katherine, and everyone would have lived happily ever after.

Dub would have married Katherine. He smiled at he thought and shook his head. She seemed more like the girl he had fallen for now than when he had tried to talk to her at the mailbox. He wondered if he had really loved her back then. Somehow, he doubted it. He told himself, if he had really loved her, he would not have left. He wondered if that was the truth or if it was just his way of justifying the mistake he had made so long ago.

"Mom have you really fallen for Mr. Taylor?" Jenn sat on the end of her mother's bed. She had driven out as soon as she had finished her last appointment. Worrying about her mother had nearly caused her to mix a client's hair dye incorrectly. Thankfully Lori had caught the mistake before she had applied it to the customer's gray roots.

"Oh, Jenn, I don't know." She had never seen her mother like this before. "I think maybe I've just gotten used to having someone pay me some attention."

Katherine was propped up against the headboard of her bed with her Bible open in her lap, just the way Jenn had found her when she got there. Jenn watched as she ran her finger down the center of it as if that would bring an answer.

"Head or heart?" Jenn did not try to hide the concern in her voice.

Katherine looked up. "What?"

Jenn smiled. "Which one is telling you it's not love?"

Katherine looked back down at the Bible and sat silent. Jenn waited.

Finally, she raised her head. "My head."

"What does your heart tell you?" Jenn tapped her chest as she asked.

She watched her mother's eyes well up with tears. Katherine placed a hand over her chest and answered, "It's telling me that I'm in trouble."

CHAPTER 24

If Dub had been willing to be honest with himself, he would have admitted that he was nervous. What had started as an I'll-show-you game had become something far more. He stood outside Katherine's house and wiped the sweat from his palms on the front of his jeans for the third time before pressing the button for the doorbell.

Feelings are for sissies, soldier, Sergeant Frye decided to make a last-minute appearance. *If you can't pull the trigger don't pick up the gun.*

Dub stepped back as the door opened and Katherine stepped out. He had never seen anyone look as beautiful as she did at that moment. The hair was different. Shorter, he thought, with more of a wave than before, and the dress she wore left him breathless. Its square neckline left enough of her chest exposed to be seductive without looking promiscuous and its hem fell just short of the top of her western boots.

"Absolutely beautiful." He bowed as he spoke.

Katherine blushed. "Jenn's idea." She curtsied. "I, myself, thought I was too old for it."

"You were wrong. Jenn was right." He offered her his arm and she took it. "I thought we'd stop for a bite to eat, if that's okay with you."

"Dairy Queen?" she laughed and gave his arm a tug.

Dub laughed. "Nope, Ole Red."

Katherine pushed what was left of her roasted turkey sandwich away and took a drink of her sweet tea. Out on a date in downtown Tishomingo, she felt like a kid again. Ole Red had not been there then, and as she thought about it, she realized the establishment's owner would have still been in elementary school when she graduated. Still, it was amazing how a couple of dates and the prospect of falling in love could wash years off of a person's soul.

Dub cut a piece from his ribeye steak and placed it in his mouth. He seemed a little distant, almost sad, she thought. "What are you thinking about?"

He finished chewing and swallowed before he spoke. "I was thinking about how so many people, myself included, don't really appreciate their lives the way they should."

"That's awful deep thinking for someone whose about to go dancing." Katherine smiled. "You want to talk about it?"

He cut the last bit of the steak into three bite-size pieces, laid the knife aside, and looked up into her eyes. "I looked into Ben's room for the first time in years yesterday. It was like stepping back in time."

"I'm so sorry." Katherine could see the pain in his eyes. "Maybe we should reschedule this date."

"No." He smiled, but she could tell it was forced, "I need something to take my mind off it. I'm sorry if I've been a little out of it."

"You know if you ever need to talk, you have my number." Deep inside she felt the urge to hold him.

His smile widened and as it did she could see the old sparkle in his eyes. "Kat, if I didn't know better, I'd think you were starting to like me a little."

She waved him off with the flip of her hand. "Different day, same old jackass. Finish your steak old man, I'm ready to dance."

The Double AA Dancehall served as a dance school Monday through Thursday. On Friday and Saturday evenings, it opened to the public. No alcohol was served or allowed on the premises. The owner, a recovering alcoholic himself, had built the place because he and his wife wanted a place they could dance and he would not have to deal with the temptations present in most of the nightclubs around the area. Dub had learned about the place from Kenneth.

The parking lot had nearly reached capacity by the time Dub parked. As soon as he opened the truck door, he heard music and the thought of twirling Katherine around the dance floor brought a smile to his face. He escorted her to the entrance and paid the cover charge. Once inside, he did not even bother to stop at a table. He led her straight to the dance floor, bowed low, pulled her in, and the two fell in with the other couples circling the room.

As they rounded the end of the dance floor, the singer broke into the song's chorus. The song seemed to be telling him to concentrate on tonight, the good times, music, laughing, and don't be worrying about tomorrow. Dub took it to heart and lost himself in the feeling of Katherine's body moving in rhythm with his. Moments of perfection in life are rare. Most people can count theirs on one hand. Dub knew this was one of his, and he found himself wishing the song would go on forever.

"That was everyone's favorite local artist, Blake Shelton, singing 'All About Tonight,' and now let's slow it down a tad," the man on the stage at the far side of the building announced. He pushed buttons on a sound system as he continued, "Ladies I think these guys would agree with George Strait when he says, 'I Just Want to Dance With You.' If any of y'all have requests, just let me know and I'll see if I can work them in."

The music started and Katherine pressed closer as they began to move to the slower beat of the new song. At the end of the floor, Dub twirled her out, stopped her on the way back, and the two continued along two-stepping side-by-side to the next corner where he gave her another twist and took the lead once more. They stayed on the floor for two more songs before Katherine said she needed a short rest.

Dub found them an empty table away from the dance floor. He pulled the seat out for her, "Would you like something to drink?"

"I would love a water." She waved a hand in front of her face trying to cool herself down.

The song that had been playing was just ending when he made it back with two bottles of water. He handed one to her and sat down in the seat behind her.

She unscrewed the top, took a drink, and then as the next song began, she leaned back towards him and raised her voice above the music. "I was thinking while you were gone, and I want to apologize for that day out by the mailbox."

"What for?" Dub sat his bottle down on the table.

"I was kind of a bitch to you," Katherine explained and turned to face him. "You know, that first time you stopped and spoke to me out by the road."

"Kat, we would not be here tonight if you had been nice." Dub grinned and winked at her.

"How do you figure?" She moved her chair closer to his.

The noise level dropped as the song ended.

"I had just come from the lawyer's office, and I stopped to tell you I was going to accept the offer you made on my property." He watched as her eyes widened. "If you had been nice, my place would already be yours and I would have been out of your hair weeks ago."

"Dub Taylor, I do not believe you!" She had to raise her voice above the beginning of the next song.

Dub held up his right hand. "I swear. You walked away that day and I just sat there in my truck thinkin', 'Well I guess I deserved that but what do I do now?' That night I was reading my Bible and the number seven caught my eye and I thought, 'Dub you don't need the money why not just make her go on seven dates with you, then she'll have to talk to you'."

"You can't be serious." Katherine shook her head.

"I'm very serious." Dub took her hand. "That's exactly where the idea came from. Now if you're ready, I'd like to dance some more."

Katherine followed as he led her back out onto the floor. As Kenny Chesney's "Me and You" started and he sang about two people in a dream that came true, she looked into his eyes. "Dub, I take back the apology. I'm so glad I was a bitch to you that day."

"I am too." He smiled. Katherine laid her head on his shoulder. He closed his eyes and prayed the Lord would allow him to hold onto this memory.

When Dub opened the truck door and helped her out, Katherine knew she was not ready for the night to end. She did not want to go on the seventh date. She did not want him to leave. Not tonight, not ever. Her mind was a mass of confused chaotic thoughts and a jumble of uncertain desires. He walked her to the front door where she fumbled with her keys, but finally managed to unlock it.

Feeling like a nervous school girl, she turned and took him by the hand. "Would you like to come in for a minute?"

He reached and took her other hand in his. "Kat, there is nothing I would like better, but I don't think it's a good idea."

"You're probably right." She looked down and hoped her disappointment did not show.

He released her left hand, placed his right hand under her chin, and raised her head until she was looking into his eyes. "It was never part of my plan to win your heart or to lose mine to you. I just wanted a chance to talk to you and apologize for being stupid and leaving. This all happened so fast and I'm afraid I'll end up hurting you again. Please know…"

"It's okay," Katherine stopped him. "It's okay."

"But I want you to know…" She placed a finger over his lips and stopped him once more.

When she was sure he would not try to continue, she removed it. "You do not need to explain. I want you to know I had a lovely evening. Quite possibly the most wonderful evening of my entire life. Thank you for that." Before he could react, she tiptoed and kissed him on the cheek before quickly turning, opening the door, and stepping inside.

"No, thank you, Kat," was the last thing she heard before the door closed.

Dub sat in his truck knowing that the minute he opened the door, the night would be over. He told himself it had been officially over when she closed the door, but some part of him refused to believe it, and so he continued to sit in the darkness and relive the night in his mind. He considered taking out his notebook and writing down as many of the night's songs as he could remember. He half expected some smart-ass remark or callused words of wisdom from Sergeant Frye, but the old marine chose to remain silent.

He leaned his head back against the headrest and closed his eyes. The image of her stepping out of her door before their date formed. He held onto it as long as he could before it started to fade away. What was it the sarge had said— *the world doesn't play fair and life sucks* —that might be true, he thought to himself, but this I brought on myself.

He opened the truck door and stepped out into the night. The cool air felt good on his face as the sound of night insects reached his ears. His old friend the barn owl hooted as if to say *you are not the only one still awake.* He walked to the door and let himself in.

Somewhere back in time, many years ago, he would have said he was home for the night. He hung his keys on a hook beside the door. Everywhere he looked there was a memory. He walked from the living room into the kitchen. The house had not felt like home in a very long time and tonight he felt a little sad because of it. Very soon it would be Katherine's and he found himself hoping that once it was hers, she would find a way to turn it back into the home it had once been.

CHAPTER 25

Katherine opened her Bible to I Corinthians 13 and looked around the room at the seven other women in her Sunday school class. She and Miz Vivian had had a long discussion before deciding to use the age of fifty as the dividing point for the new class. Miz Vivian had taken those above and she those below. The oldest of the ladies in Katherine's class, not including herself, was forty-seven and the youngest twenty-six.

Last week's class had been more of a get-to-know-everyone event than an actual Bible study, but this week Katherine found herself eager to really dive into scriptures. For years she had disliked this particular chapter, "the love chapter" some called it. She was not sure if she would be able to express what had changed within herself or how she had come to understand and appreciate the way the verses explained love, but she knew she must try.

Someone knocked softly on the classroom door and then opened it. Judi, the young woman Katherine and Dub had visited with at the Dairy Queen, stepped in followed by Brother Jerry.

"This young lady informed me that she was your guest," he spoke to Katherine from the doorway. "I wanted to thank you for inviting her."

Katherine was not sure how to respond, so she simply nodded and said as Judi entered the room and took a seat, "Everyone this is Judi. She is a student at the college."

A round of introductions and questions about her major filled the next several minutes. As Katherine watched and listened, the verse from Matthew about putting one's lamp under a bushel, came to her mind. The thought of the years she had hidden herself away and the time she had wasted pricked her heart, and she promised herself it would never happen again.

Katherine asked for the ladies' attention before she began. "For many years, I did not know what love was, and if I'm honest, there are still times I'm not sure if I've got it right. In this chapter, Paul gives an explanation, but first let's look at the three verses leading up to his description of love."

As the others flipped their Bibles open, Katherine continued, "The first verse tells us that if we don't have love in us, then the words we speak, no matter how eloquent, are nothing more than noise. As I look back over my own life, it pains me to admit it, but too much of what came out of my mouth was the worst kind of racket possible and most of the time I turned the volume to its maximum in an attempt to be heard."

Katherine noticed a couple of the others nodding in agreement. "I have learned that people are more inclined to listen to you when you whisper. That is not to say that I always whisper. There are still times when my temper takes over, and, well you get the picture."

For the next half hour, Katherine led the class in an in-depth discussion of the first three verses of the chapter. When the time drew near for the class to end, she realized they had not even touched on the love verses and made a mental note to visit with Miz Vivian and Brother Jerry about the possibility of staying with this chapter instead of moving on to the next one the following Sunday.

As the ladies filed out the door, Judi stopped her. "Mrs. Katherine, I just wanted to thank you again for inviting me. You don't know how much I need this in my life right now."

"Judi, my dear child," Katherine put her arm across Judi's shoulder, "I understand completely. If it had not been for Dub, I would still be hid away at home, hiding my light under my bed."

Judi laughed. "Now that would be an awful shame because I really enjoyed your class."

"Thank you." Katherine guided her along the hall towards the sanctuary. "Hearing that is like music to my heart."

"Speaking of hearts," Judi winked at her and asked, "where is Mr. Taylor?"

Dub sat at home with his Bible in his lap. He had just read through the twentieth chapter of Matthew. He thought about Jesus's parable of the laborers in the first sixteen verses. This parable and that of the prodigal son gave him hope. Most days it extinguished the fires of doubt that cropped up whenever his mind turned to the evil he had been part of in the past. Today the flames seemed to be fighting harder than usual and so he bowed his head and prayed.

When he raised his head several minutes later, he closed his Bible and set it aside. He pulled the notebook from his shirt pocket and flipped through it until he found the sheet with his list of churches. He felt a bit guilty as he pulled the page out. The Baptist church was the next one on the list and if he had not felt so unsocial, he would have attended it this morning.

He would miss the sermons when he left, at least for a little while, he thought. He laid a hand on the Bible and felt the comfort of it. So many wasted years, once again doubt sparked. He smiled and thanked his parents for the way they had raised him. "*And when he is old, he will not depart from it,*" the Proverb crossed his mind. But he had departed from it for all those years. Not just departed from it, but ran from it, hid from it. The last part of the fourteenth verse of Matthew 20 brought a weak smile. "*I will give unto this last, even as unto thee.*" Dub found himself hoping as he rose from his seat that he had indeed done enough to be counted among the last.

In the kitchen he tossed the sheet from his notebook into the trash. He leaned against the counter and looked at the eight boxes on the table. The photographs he wanted from them were at his new home. He had yet to come to a decision on what to do with those left. Both of his parents had been only children. Somewhere out in the world, he had distant relatives but none of them he knew and none who would be interested in these pictures. With the exception of those from the homecoming game, he had given Katherine all of the pictures with her and Vickie in them. He could not bear the thought of destroying them. No other idea came to mind, so he stacked them into one tall tower of boxes and took them into his parent's room and returned them to the place he had found them on the top shelf of their closet.

Katherine's eyes scanned the sanctuary looking for Dub. When she realized he was not there, disappointment set in and she was even more glad that Judi had decided to attend. As the two settled into a pew near the back of the room, Katherine patted Judi on the knee. "Thank you again for coming this morning and I hope you'll consider coming again."

"I will." Judi smiled.

Brother Jerry stepped to the pulpit and asked everyone to bow their heads. He prayed for the congregation and for the Lord to help him deliver the message. When he finished praying, the congregation said "Amen", but before Katherine joined hers with the rest of the congregation, she whispered, "And Lord, please watch over Dub."

When Jenn arrived at her mother's house, she found Katherine in the game room. "Pizza and pop, just like you ordered." she held the food up. "Are we eating in here or in the kitchen?"

"In here, I think," Katherine said as she took the painting of her and Dub on the tailgate of his father's old truck off the easel and switched it for the one of the six cowboys peeing.

Jenn placed the cardboard box that housed the pizza on the far end of the pool table and came back to stand beside her mother. She watched as Katherine painted KAT in a red-brick color on the bottom right corner of the canvas.

"I didn't think you liked being called Kat." Jenn pointed at the signature.

"I guess it has grown on me," Katherine said as she swirled the brush in a jelly jar of mineral spirits.

Jenn looked over her mother's shoulder at the painting Katherine had hung on the wall. "And just who would those kids in the back of that truck be?" She pointed at it.

Katherine smiled. "Those kids would be me and Dub a very long time ago."

"No way," Jenn spoke as she moved to get a better view.

"Yes, way," Katherine giggled, laid the brush on an old rag to dry, and stepped up beside her daughter.

That her mother could paint at all was incredible to Jenn. How and why Katherine had kept her talent hidden all these years Jenn did not know and could not understand. As she studied the lines and details in her mother's newest work of art, she was truly impressed. "Mom, you are very talented. These paintings are very good. I bet if you wanted to sell them you could get a bit of money for them."

"Oh, no, they are not for sale," Katherine turned back to the pool table and left Jenn staring at the painting. She flipped the lid back on the cardboard box and took out a piece of pizza.

The smell of pizza spread through the room attempting without success to drown out the harsh tang of paint and mineral spirits that had taken up residence. Unable to completely do so, it reached Jenn as a mixture of the three. The hiss of escaping carbonation as Katherine screwed the cap off one of the soft drinks, along with the aroma of the food reminded Jenn that she had skipped breakfast and needed sustenance.

"This house is big enough you shouldn't have any trouble finding a place to hang them," Jenn said as she searched for the biggest piece of pizza. "You could always hang the one of the guys peeing above the toilet in the guest bathroom."

Katherine chuckled. "That's not a bad idea. I like it."

"I'm not sure where I'd put this one." Jenn pointed at the other painting.

Katherine finished chewing the pizza in her mouth and swallowed. "I thought I might give that one to Dub."

Jenn laid her piece of pizza on the tarp covering the table and opened her drink, "Date number six must have gone quite well."

"It went very well," Katherine nodded before taking another bite.

Jenn looked at her mother. The glow was there, that visible shine that a person gets when they begin to have feelings for someone. She reminded herself that this was not exactly a stranger, her mother and Dub had come close to a relationship before, and had fate not interfered, he could have very easily been her father. Even with that knowledge, Jenn could not help but feel apprehensive. "You're falling for Mr. Taylor aren't you, Mom?"

"I'm not sure." Katherine shrugged. "Everything just seems to be happening so fast. I can't seem to wrap my mind around it."

"Speaking of Mr. Taylor," Jenn tossed the crust that was left from her pizza back into the box, "you really scared Lori last week when she asked you what you were going to do with his land once he was gone. What was all of that about?"

Katherine shook her head. "I don't know. The question caught me off guard. I've been... well, you could say I've been hiding from life for so long that sometimes I just don't think past today. Until Lori asked me, I had not even considered that Dub would be leaving after our seventh date. I'm not sure what I thought he was going to do but, in my mind, it did not involve him not being around."

Jenn took a drink and tried to think of something helpful to say. She was worried and wanted to guide Katherine, but she also remembered how badly her one and only marriage had been. She had ignored all of the many red flags and when her mother had tried to warn her, she had ignored her also. She knew wisdom was not her strong suit, but she suppressed her feelings of inadequacy. "Mom, I don't want to see you get hurt again. I don't know Mr. Taylor all that well and I'm sure he's a nice man, but promise me you'll be careful."

Katherine looked at her and smiled. "I will."

The two of them leaned against the pool table and finished another piece of pizza each before Jenn spoke again. "You still haven't answered the question of what you are going to do with Mr. Taylor's land."

Katherine added her crust to the three that were already in the box. "Tomorrow I have to meet him at the lawyer's office to discuss our seventh date. I'm planning on seeing if he will visit with me afterwards about changing the terms of our deal."

"Changing them how?" Jenn turned to look at her mother.

Katherine was staring past her at the painting of her and Dub. "I'm going to ask him to at least keep the twenty acres and his house. I want him to stay."

Lord help her and Lord help Mr. Taylor, Jenn thought to herself.

CHAPTER 26

Dub was standing beside his pickup early Monday morning when a white van pulled up beside him, "Mr. Taylor?"

Dub looked up at the young man behind the wheel, "Present and accounted for. And you would be?"

"Darion, sir." the driver smiled and opened his door. He reminded Dub of a young man he had trained with years ago, same good-natured sparkle in the eyes, same height and build. Dub tried to remember the kid's name and could not.

"Darion, just so we're clear, I am not an officer." Dub drew his eyebrows down hard, "And I realize that there is also the chance that you are speaking out of respect for my age, but young man, I am not old, so we will be leaving off with the 'sir' shit. Are we clear?"

"Yes, sir," Darion responded before thinking and then stammered, "sorry, I mean, yes, Mr. Taylor."

"Mr. Taylor was my father." Dub held up his duffle. "Call me Dub. Where should I stow my gear?"

Darion slid the side door of the van open. "Wherever you'd like Dub. It's just you and me today, so you get your pick of seats also."

"Don't reckon you're allowed to let me drive," Dub said as he tossed his duffle on the floor behind the driver's seat.

Darion chuckled. "That would be a solid no, sir... sorry, Dub."

Dub smiled, "Then I guess I'll take the passenger's seat. I'm not much for riding in the back of vehicles. Seen one too many soldiers trapped inside."

Darion gave a solemn nod, slid the door shut, and pulled himself back up behind the wheel. Dub made his way around to the passenger's side and stood for a long minute looking out past the barn at the land before opening the door and stepping up into his seat. "Onward and upward."

Darion, who had been watching him, gave him a confused look. "What do you mean by that, sir?"

As he started to stammer an apology, Dub shook his head. "Darion, you've got a lot to learn and a long way to go. The bigger problem, as I see it, is time is short. Time is very short."

"Does that mean you're ready to go?" Darion asked, much to Dub's amusement.

"That would be a solid yes." Dub chuckled.

Darion backed up, got the van headed in the right direction, and started down the gravel lane. Through the side mirror, Dub watched the house recede until they made a turn, and it was no longer visible.

"What's today's mission?" Dub looked at Darion once he could no longer see the house.

Darion pulled to a stop at the end of the driveway, looked both ways, and turned right, "My orders are to take you to see your specialist and then it's on to the center to get you checked in proper like."

Dub held up a keyring. "I'm gonna need to add a stop to that directive, soldier. I've got to drop these at my lawyer's office."

"Mr. Taylor, I mean, Dub," Darion kept his eyes on the road as he spoke, "I'm not military. I never served."

"Just a figure of speech." Dub chuckled. "But I do need to make that stop. Any reason why that can't happen?"

"None that I can think of." Darion shook his head. "Just tell me when to turn."

Katherine spent her first waking hour trying to figure out what she was going to say to Dub. The bowl of oatmeal she made herself for breakfast was a waste of time. She stirred it around while she attempted a few dialogues in her head. Each one ran its course and ended with her feeling like a stuttering schoolgirl. If she could not do it in her head, how was she ever going to manage it in person? Frustrated, she scraped the cold clump of oats into the sink, started the water flowing, and turned on the garbage disposal.

This could be a metaphor for my life, she thought as she watched her breakfast disappear down the drain. Just like Goldilocks, it's too hot or too cold until it's just right and then everything goes to hell. When the last of the oatmeal was gone, she turned off the disposal and water and returned to her room.

The Bible on her nightstand caught her eye. *The answer to every question can be found right here,* the words came with the memory of her mother holding an old worn Bible in her hands. *You may have to search for it, but I guarantee it's in here.* Katherine smiled, settled on the bed, and picked the Bible up.

She hoped for the Lord's guidance as she set the Bible on its spine and randomly allowed it to fall open. When she looked, the page in front of her was the love chapter, I Corinthians 13. Her first thought was that it happened because that was the last place she had been reading but as she started to pick the Bible up, the words, "Love never fails", flashed across her vision and she stopped.

Never fails, she read again. But was this love or something else? If it was love, she reasoned, then what I say and how I say it does not matter as long as I say it with love in my heart. She went back to the beginning and read the chapter through completely. Still not certain she had an answer, she placed the Bible back on the nightstand.

Worrying about it was getting her nowhere, she decided. She would get herself ready for the meeting and surely something would come to her by the time she saw Dub there, and if it did not then, well, she would just have to improvise.

"Are you sure about this?" Mason looked up at Dub from his seat as he took the keyring from his client.

"I've never been more sure of anything in my life." Dub smiled and eased down into his usual seat. "Is everything in order? Anything else you need me to sign?"

Mason had been hoping there would be a change of heart. In part because he wanted to see how the story would play out but also because he was not looking forward to having to meet with Katherine Williams alone. He made a show of shuffling through the papers in the folder on his desk, the same documents he had looked over at least four times already.

"Everything is just as you wanted it arranged. There is nothing further to sign." He placed everything back into the folder and looked up. "I think we're all good, Mr. Taylor."

Dub took in a deep breath then let it out slowly. "Feels good knowing she's going to have the old place. Thank you, and, Mason, I think it's about time we dropped the Mr. Taylor nonsense. Hell, you were a grade ahead of me the whole time we were going to school. Ben would have graduated with you if he had lived."

Mason had never really liked Ben. One of the many cases of "I play sports and you don't" that separate so many people in school. There had never been any real problems, just a few off-handed remarks here and there. Mason had learned early on to keep his distance and ignore Ben.

That Dub had chosen him had been a bit of a shock. He was fairly certain Dub knew that Ben and he had a problem back before the accident and still Dub had shown up at his office asking for his help. He had considered lying and saying his plate was full. He was glad now that he had not.

"Alright, Dub." Mason was not in the habit of calling his clients by their first names and even now with permission it sounded strange to him. "I have one question."

"Shoot." Nonchalantly, Dub spoke the single word. The ease and simplicity of the way the man did everything, Mason found admirable. Dub had been a quiet person even back when they attended school. Since the day Dub had retained his services, he had noticed how efficient his client was and on several occasions had wondered if his military training had anything to do with it. Mason wished he was a bit more like Dub.

"Of all the lawyers available, why did you pick me to represent you?" Mason laid a hand on the file on his desk as he asked the question.

Dub leaned back in his chair and rubbed his thumb along the side of his jaw. "Mason, my brother was an asshole. Because he was my brother, I loved him in spite of that fact; however, I have very few memories of Ben in which I actually liked him. I remember the way he treated you and the few other guys who did not play sports, and so did not live up to his measurement of what a man should be. I never understood or agreed with his way of thinking. You were one of the hardest working students in the school. Except for athletics, if I remember correctly, you were in just about every other organization the school offered for guys and the way you handled Ben's attitude and others like him, well, I always found that to be impressive."

Mason was fairly certain that if a man his size could float, he would be looking down at Dub from the ceiling. Dub continued, "When I decided to donate my land to the state, you were the first one I thought of and as it turned out, it was a good thing. I don't think there is another lawyer in this town, maybe even this state, who could have dealt with Kat as well as you did. And for that my friend, I am eternally in your debt."

Mason sat silent and allowed what Dub had said to sink in completely. It had been a long time since anyone made him feel good about himself and it felt... well, it felt good. He took his hand from the folder and ran it across the top of his balding head. "One more question?"

Dub simply nodded this time.

"Why is it so important to you that the land goes to Mrs. Williams?" Mason pulled at his ear as he spoke. "Do you not have any kinfolks who might want it?"

With a smile Dub leaned forward and tapped a knuckle on the top of the desk, "Mr. Counselor, I find it necessary to inform you that that was indeed two questions." He chuckled and sat back in his chair. "I think I shall answer the second one first. No, I do not think any of my kinfolk will want this land. As a matter of fact, I would not even know where to find any of my kin. Both of my parents were only children. I'm sure I have distant cousins out there somewhere but who knows? And so, that brings us to your other question. My family and Kat's family lived side by side from the time I can remember. I don't know if she had cousins or kin. If she did, I never met them. Anyway, Kat and I may not be blood kin but in my mind, she is about the closest to kin that I know."

Mason had been the middle child of five. An older brother and sister and two younger sisters had rounded out his siblings. His father's family had four kids in it and his mother's three. At family gatherings there were times he sometimes had to ask who was who. It had never occurred to him that there were people in the world with no family and while he felt empathy for Dub in the matter, he also felt very blessed.

"I see." He nodded as Dub stood up.

"My driver's waiting." Dub stuck his hand across the desk, "I sure appreciate all you've done for me."

Mason rose and shook Dub's hand. "It has been my pleasure, Dub."

"You say that now," Dub chuckled as they released hands, "but Kat will be here shortly and then we'll see how much of a pleasure it is. I'll go ahead and apologize now. I'm sorry to put you in this situation, but I think it's better that I'm not here when you tell her about the seventh date."

Mason continued to stand as Dub walked to the door. As he always did, he retrieved his Stetson from the hat rack and settled it on his head before reaching for the door. Then he opened the door. But before he stepped out, he turned back. "Mason, one last thing. I want you to know something—you are stronger than you

177

think you are." And with that he stepped out and closed the door behind him.

Mason smiled. *You may be right, Dub,* he thought, *but as you said, Mrs. Williams will be here soon and you can bet your ass, she's going to put that theory to the test.*

CHAPTER 27

Katherine arrived early, far earlier than the time she normally did. She realized as she sat in her car and stared out the window at the empty parking spaces around her that this was the first time she had arrived before Dub. She had never liked being early, nor did she like being late. Her ex-husband's adage that if you were not there fifteen minutes prior to the set time then you were late was one of the many things they had never agreed on and fashionably late was an oxymoron to her. No, she preferred to walk in the door at the exact time specified, but if that was not possible, she was comfortable being three to five minutes early.

The clock on the dash indicated it was twelve twenty-three. Over half an hour until their appointment. There was no way she was going to be able to sit in her car that long without making herself crazy. She considered driving around the block to the Dairy Queen but decided it would be pointless seeing that she did not really want anything. Another five minutes crawled past before she finally opened her door and stepped out of the car.

With no plan and no destination in mind, she locked it and walked away. The parking lot ended, and she stepped up onto the sidewalk. A right would take her to Mason's office, but it was still too early, so she turned left instead. A block away was one of the Pennington Creek crossings. This one had separate bridges for pedestrians and vehicles.

Several cars and a truck drove by as she made her way to the creek. Once there she continued out onto the walking bridge. Halfway to the other side she stopped and stared over the railing into the water below. The movement of her shadow on the water caused several turtles to slide off the rock they were basking on into the water. As the last of them disappeared from her sight under the bridge, she recalled a time when she and Vickie had stood in this very spot and tossed pieces of bread over the railing to the perch below. Back then the bridge behind her had been an old wooden suspension bridge.

She tried to remember when exactly a flood had taken it out. If her memory served her right, it had been close to the time when Dub had left for the military. The concrete bridge that stood in its place was not nearly as picturesque, but, in her opinion, more enjoyable to cross. She had never liked the old single lane structure with its cables and wooden driving surface. The way it had swayed and the thump-thump of the vehicle tires moving from one slat to the next had always made her heart drop into her stomach, much like the thought of asking Dub to stay was doing now.

"Mr. Taylor, the doctor will see you now," the nurse that spoke was one Dub had not seen on any of his previous visits. She was young with dark shoulder-length hair and a warm caring smile.

Dub followed her down the hall. She stopped beside a set of scales and instructed him to step onto them. He did as instructed and watched as she wrote the weight on his chart before pointing him to an open door a little further down the hall. Once inside, she took his temperature and blood pressure. When she was finished, she smiled.

"All good. The doctor will be with you shortly," she spoke as she pulled the door shut behind her.

Alone with his thoughts, he stared around the room until his eyes stopped on the "Understanding Alzheimer's Disease" poster on the far wall. It had been four years since a doctor affiliated with the Military and Veterans Health Institute out of Johns Hopkins University had diagnosed him with the disease. He wished he could remember the doctor's name. The counselor who had been helping him with his post-traumatic stress disorder had referred him, another name he had lost.

The door opened and Doctor Lee entered. Dub smiled and wondered how long it would be until he would have to add him to the forgotten-names list.

"How is Mr. Taylor doing today?" he flipped through a chart as he asked.

"I'm still kickin'." Dub looked up at him, "Just don't ask me to name what I'm kickin' at."

Doctor Lee pushed the room's rolling stool to the wall-attached desk and placed the open chart down before seating himself. "It's good to see you still have your humor about you, Mr. Taylor. I've been looking at the last set of tests. I'm afraid the news is not what we had hoped it would be. The new medicine is not working any better than the last two did and I'm afraid we've run out of options."

"So much for the good news." Dub watched as his doctor shook his head. "What's the bad news, doc?"

"Mr. Taylor in all my years, I have never had a patient quite like you." He removed his glasses and rubbed his eyes, "The bad news is that both your blood test and your last CT scan indicate an increase in the rate of the disease's progression. How have you been sleeping?"

Dub ran his finger along the edge of his chin. "About like usual, I have good days and bad days. I have noticed it's getting harder to remember things. I have to check my notebook more often now."

The doctor picked the chart up and flipped through it once more. Dub watched and waited. Death did not scare him. He had wished for it too many times over the years and now that he neared the end, his only wish was that he had done enough good to amend for all of the bad in his life. There were those who had told him all he had to do was repent and ask for forgiveness. He hoped that there was truth in their words. His greatest fear was that the disease had taken some memory from him, some sin he could no longer recall, and therefore could not repent of and ask forgiveness.

"The man who first diagnosed me told me I had eleven years if my luck held." Dub watched the doctor run a finger down one edge of his chart. "That was four years ago. That I can remember, the doctor's name not so much."

Doctor Lee's finger stopped moving and he tapped at a line on the paper. "If you're asking me how much longer you have, Mr. Taylor, I cannot tell you. Each case is individual, and I won't say your forgotten doctor was wrong, but eleven years is more of an average than a given."

"So, what can you tell me?" Dub asked as he pulled out his notebook.

Doctor Lee tapped the line once more. "You score on the MMSE test has fallen another two points. The last time we visited, you were considering looking a place you could get help."

"I'm headed there as soon as we're done here." Dub flipped the notebook open, "Here is my new address if you need it."

Doctor Lee rolled his chair across the room and copied the address onto the bottom of Dub's chart. "Sulphur Veterans Center. I think this is a very wise decision, Mr. Taylor."

Dub's truck was still not in the parking area when Katherine made it back from her little stroll to the creek. She checked the time on her phone once more before crossing to her car. Had she gotten the time wrong, she wondered as she opened the door and eased into the driver's seat. Her purse was in the passenger floorboard where she had left it. She retrieved it and took out her appointment book. A quick check told her she had the time right so where was Dub? She shoved the book back into the purse, dropped the purse back into the floor, and stepped back out of the vehicle. Confused and a bit worried, she closed the door and started across the lot.

Dub pulled his seatbelt around and strapped it in place as Darion started the van. He was exhausted. It was the main reason he disliked doctor's visits. There was just something about them that wore him out both mentally and physically. He checked his watch. It was three minutes until one o'clock. Katherine would be walking in the door at Mason's office any time now if she had not already. His chest felt heavy, like a large stone was lodged against his heart. He wondered if it was because of the news he had just received, or if it was for the news Mason was about to give Katherine. He was a bit worried for Mason, but deep inside he knew the hurt was for himself and for Kat.

CHAPTER 28

Katherine pushed the door open and stepped into Mason's office. Dub's hat was not on the rack where it should be, and Dub was not in the chair where he should be either. Something was not right, and Katherine felt a sudden urge to turn and run. To sprint to her car, drive home without stopping, and just disappear once more into the hole that had been her life before Dub had shown up.

Instead, she crossed to the chair she now thought of as hers and sat down. "I guess Dub is running late." She refused to give up hope.

"Mrs. Williams, I am sorry to be the one to give you this news," Mason's voice seemed odd as he spoke, "but Mr. Taylor will not be joining us today. He asked me to... to. I'm sorry, I have never been in this position before and I don't know exactly what to say."

Katherine felt numb. She waited while Mason opened the file folder on the desk in front of him and took out the top sheet of paper. "I made some notes." he looked over the top of the single page at her. "But now I don't know where to start."

"I find it best to start at the beginning." Katherine's heart felt like it was about to stop beating one second and then the next it pumped so hard she was afraid it would burst.

"The beginning." Mason laid the paper aside. "Dub, Mr. Taylor, came to me a few months ago and asked me to arrange for his property to be donated to the state of Oklahoma as part of the Tishomingo refuge. I thought it was an odd request, but at his insistence, I agreed to do it. While I was still in the process of getting the paperwork together, you showed up here and made a monetary offer on the land."

Katherine was not sure where this was going, but she had advised him to start at the beginning, so she held her peace as he continued. "When I extended your offer to Dub, he laughed and shook his head. I told him to think about it at least overnight before he made his decision. When he left here that day, I was pretty sure he was going to refuse your offer, so when he showed up the next day and said he had a counteroffer, I was more than a little surprised. But when he gave me the details of the counteroffer, I thought he had lost his mind."

Katherine nodded. "The seven dates." She too had thought he was absolutely crazy.

"Yes, the seven dates." Mason opened the file folder once more and laid a set of papers on the edge of the desk. "I had to do some real digging and get a couple of others' opinions before I even knew if what he was asking was legal. I did not know at the time of his condition."

"Condition?" Katherine fought the urge to scream. "What condition?"

"Mrs. Williams, Dub has Alzheimer's," Mason looked like he was having trouble holding it together himself as he continued. "I did not know until after you left the office following the fifth date."

Katherine closed her eyes and willed herself to stay calm. The questions bombarding her mind came in waves. She tried to sort them but could not. She tried to pick the most important one but could not figure out which one that one would be, so she opened her eyes and picked up the paper Mason had placed on the desk in front of her. It was the agreement she had signed.

"So, is this binding?" She asked the question that came to the forefront.

"It is," Mason assured her. "Mr. Taylor, Dub, is nothing if not thorough. Unbeknownst to me, he went through the processes to ensure he had the proper documents stating he was of sound mind and body before he signed that contract. He produced them and gave me a copy after you left our last meeting." Mason dug another set of papers out of the folder and passed them across to her.

"The seventh date?" Katherine laid both sets of papers back on the desk. "What about the seventh date?"

Mason handed her an envelope and laid a set of keys on the desk in front of her. "Dub told me to give these to you when you arrived. I have not read what is inside, but he assured me it would explain his wishes."

Her heart threatened to explode. She looked at the envelope and then back to Mason. "Do I open this now."

"I believe you should, yes." He held up another set of papers. "I do not know how to proceed until I know your plans."

Her hands shook as she opened the envelope and took out the single sheet of paper. Handwritten, it read:

Dear Katherine,

It is my deepest wish that you have the house and land that once was my family's home. I have already apologized for the mistakes I made in the past with regards to you and so do not feel the need to repeat them here. I hope you know that I was sincere. It has been a pleasure, over the last six dates, to see you return to the beautiful person I knew so long ago. It is my greatest hope that you will continue to grow and flourish. I want you to know that I would very much have liked to have "won your heart" but as you have at this point undoubtably been told by Mason of my condition, doing so would have led to me hurting you once more. And that I could not, would not, do. In return, I ask that you honor our agreement. I do not know the hour or day of our seventh date but if you agree to it, Mason has the details. In closing, I want you to know that the most precious memories I have of my life are those which include you. I do not know what the future holds for me, but if I get a choice, my memories of you will be the last to go.

Your Favorite Jackass,
Dub Taylor

The ache in her heart threatened to choke her as tears flowed freely down her cheeks. She heard Mason open a desk drawer. When she looked up, he held out a box of tissues to her. She took several. As she wiped her eyes, she watched Mason do the same and wondered if Dub had this effect on everyone he met.

When the two of them had composed themselves once again, Katherine put the letter back into its envelope and laid it on the pile of papers in front of her. "Dub says you have the details of the seventh date."

Mason ran a hand across his forehead. "He has prepared a statement to be read at a graveside service once he has passed. Everything has been arranged for the ceremony. It will be very simple, and I don't expect very many folks to show up. Dub's words not mine. He would like you to read the statement and if you would like to say a few words."

"And if I do not agree to do so?" Katherine wiped away a new set of tears.

"Dub said you would ask me that." Mason smiled, but she could see the pain behind it, "He told me to tell you, whether you agreed or not, that the land, the house, and the truck were all yours, and he hoped you could live knowing that you had welched on the deal."

Katherine took the keys from the edge of the desk and held them in her hands. "The truck was not part of the deal."

"He said you would say that too." Mason shook his head. "He said to tell you he could not have it where he was going, and he thought you would look much better in it than that damn thing you've been driving around."

187

Katherine touched each key, first the truck key and then the house key. The fob on the ring was the marine ensign. She ran her thumb over it. "Do you know where it is that he was going?"

Mason did not hesitate to say, "The Veteran's Center in Sulphur. He stopped this morning and dropped those keys off."

"Did he leave any further instructions?" Katherine placed the keys on top of the papers in front of her.

"No, he did not." Mason looked from her to the keys. "There are a few papers for you to sign and some minor details to attend to, and then the property is yours. Would you like to do that now or should we wait until a later date?"

Katherine leaned forward. "Don't you need to know if I agree to the seventh date, first?"

Mason rubbed the back of his neck and shook his head. "No. At this point, it does not make a difference one way or another. When the time comes, I will call you. Dub left it up to me to take care of everything. At that time if you wish to fulfill your agreement with Dub, then…"

"And if I refuse to sign the papers that give me ownership of the property," Katherine's mind raced, "what then?"

Mason hung his head. "I don't think I have ever wished harder that someone would be wrong in all my life." He looked back up into Katherine's eyes. "Dub said you would ask that question also. He said if you refused to finalize the paperwork then I was to get the papers ready to donate the land to the state and he would find a way to get them signed."

It was too much. She felt like life had backed her into a corner and if she came out swinging it was likely to knock her out cold. Her mind and body already ached from the steady stream of emotions running through them. The thought of throwing a fit, maybe scream at Mason a little, crossed her mind, but looking at him, she could see he was on the ropes himself. He did not seem to be pushing her to make a swift decision.

"How long do I have to decide?" She waved a hand over the stack in front of her.

"There is no set timetable," Mason said, "but I would advise not to wait too long. Dub wants you to have the property and for now he is still in control of his mental facilities; however, in time that may change."

"Would the end of the week be too long?" Katherine asked.

"Under the circumstances, I would think not." Mason scratched the side of his neck, "I think you should go ahead and take the keys though. Perhaps even take a look at the property before you decide."

Katherine stood, gathered the papers and the keys, and asked, "Have you ever hated someone so much that you love them?"

Mason looked up at her, a smile on his face. "In all my life I have never seen anything like what you and Dub have. It's like watching fire and water dance. It's both beautiful and scary at the same time."

Katherine smiled, "Thank you, Mason. I know this could not have been easy for you."

For a long time after Katherine shut the door behind her, Mason sat at his desk and stared at the chair Dub usually sat in. As if life was not confusing enough, fate had seen fit to drop Dub Taylor and Katherine Williams into his lap. It was not that he had been all that happy with his life, but there was comfort in the known. He smoked too much. Drank too often. Cursed the life that had been chosen for him. And wondered if there truly was a God, why he had never been able to find peace.

Dub Taylor seemed to be at peace. A man with a disease that would surely kill him before too much longer, yet there was a calmness within him that Mason did not have and could not understand. He spent his days in the bottle because the church he had been raised in had not brought about the peace he searched for, and the more he had read the Bible, the more confused he had become.

Mason picked up the file folder from his desk, stood up, and took it with him to the file cabinet. The hope he had found in Dub and Katherine's relationship had vanished. No sign would be given now. He opened the drawer, placed the file in its place, and picked up the bottle and glass. Back at his desk he poured the glass half full. *To hope,* he raised the glass in toast, *and all the fools like me who refuse to let it go.*

CHAPTER 29

Tuesday morning Dub opened his eyes and stared at the ceiling. He remembered his name, where he was, and he was fairly certain it was Tuesday. He pushed himself up in the bed, reached for his cellphone, and checked the time and date, then chuckled. It was strange the way the mind will mess with a person. Somewhere in his brain, he figured there must be a tiny closet with a little brass name plate that had written on it — Stupid Thoughts.

Over the last several weeks, the door had been opened just enough to let one of those crazy little critters loose. It had half convinced him that as soon as he moved into the Veteran's Center, his mind would instantly deteriorate. Even knowing what he knew about the way the disease progressed, he had allowed the notion to settle in and had resigned himself to the idea when he awoke, he would remember nothing.

He tossed the covers off, threw his legs over the edge of the bed, stood up, and stretched. Home, sweet, home, not unlike so many he had known in his years on this earth. A tad smaller than some and much larger than others. A one-man tent and a lean-to made of pine boughs came to mind. He had been snowed in, he remembered. He tried to recall when and where it had been and could not.

As he made the bed, he ran through a mental regimen he had started at some point. My name is Dub Tayor. I am fifty-eight. I grew up in Tishomingo, Oklahoma. I spent... twenty-something years in the Marines. During the Gulf War, I served in... he paused and waited. When it would not come, he moved on. When I retired, I traveled. I have been in every state in the U.S., all...

191

once again the information would not come. Frustrated, he picked up the spiral notebook off his nightstand, flipped it open and searched until he found the page which listed the military conflicts he had served in. The page after had a list of the countries he had visited overseas and the one after that, he had listed all fifty U.S. states. He ran his finger along each page before closing it and laying it back in its place.

Opening the closet, he laid out his clothes for the day and then stepped into the small bathroom. As he undressed, Sergeant Frye's voice filled his head, *Shit, shower, and shave. Get the three S's out of the way and you're ready for the day.*

He shook his head and turned on the shower. Why could he remember every asinine thing the sarge had ever said, but he could not remember how many states were in the union? He tested the water, stepped in, and pulled the curtain across. As the water soaked his hair and ran down his body, he wondered if he should add a new page of notes to his morning regimen. A page dedicated to Kat for when he truly began to forget.

"I don't know what to do." Katherine sat beside Vivian on the couch in the parsonage.

She had spent most of the morning wandering through her house trying to wrap her mind around the news she had been given. Unable to do so, she had set with her Bible. When she picked it up the plan was to read it but twenty minutes later it was still laying open on her lap in front of her on the counter and she had done nothing but stare at the same two pages.

Desperate for answers she had driven into town and poured her heart out to Vivian, who had sat quietly and listened. Katherine could feel the pressure of emotions building in her chest as she looked to the lady beside her for answers.

Vivian took her hand, "My grandmother used to tell me that a person could eat an elephant one bite at a time."

Katherine was not sure this was the kind of answer she was looking for but sat patiently while Vivian continued, "Child you are dealing with a lot and while it is all connected, it needs to be processed bit by bit."

"But where do I start?" Katherine found strength in just holding Vivian's hand.

"At the beginning." Vivian smiled.

Brother Jerry came from the back of the house and stopped at the end of the house, "I'm going over to the office to work on tomorrow's sermon. Do you ladies need anything before I go?"

Katherine shook her head. Vivian looked past her and smiled. "I think we're okay, honey."

Katherine waited until she heard a door close before she spoke. "I found out that Dub was back in town and planning to sell the land his family had leased to my family, well to me, since my parents are gone now, and I bought out my sister."

Vivian held up a finger and indicated for Katherine to stop. Katherine paused, confused, and looked at her.

"I do not think that is the beginning." Vivian lowered her finger and stared into Katherine's eyes. Katherine felt as if Vivian was staring straight into her very soul.

"I don't understand." Katherine wanted to look away but did not.

Vivian released Katherine's hand and turned as far as the walking boot on her foot would allow. "It is my understanding that you and Dub knew each other as kids. Let's start there."

Katherine began to think that it had been a mistake to come but since she was already here, she took a second to regroup before she started again. "Our families owned land that adjoined. My parents had two children, me, and my older sister. Dub's parents had two boys. He was the younger of the two. We grew up together."

"And what was it that drew you to Dub?" Vivian interrupted.

Katherine felt herself flush. This was not the conversation

she had planned to have with the pastor's wife. She simply wanted to know whether she should take possession of the land and what to do about the way she felt about Dub.

When she did not answer, Vivian leaned closer. "Was it his looks? Or was he the only boy that showed you attention? What drew you to him?"

Katherine searched her brain trying to find a one-word answer so they could move on to a more comfortable topic. Dub had been a good-looking guy, still was for that matter, but that was not what had drawn her to him. He was also not the only one who had shown an interest in her back then so that was not the reason.

She took a breath in through her nose and slowly released it. "Dub was very handsome but that is not why I was interested in him. And he was not the only one interested in me. Part of it was what we shared. We used to call it our shadow-complex. Both of us felt like we were living in our older siblings' shadows. He was my best friend. I could talk to him about anything."

"You were just friends then?" It seemed to Katherine that Vivian's questions were pushing her but was not sure she like the direction, "Best friends but just friends?"

"For a very brief time, we were more than friends." Katherine hoped that would end this line of questioning.

"So, you were lovers?" Vivian's question hung in the air between them. It was not an accusation but more of an inquiry.

"Oh, Lord, no," Katherine gasped, "we never... I mean one night we kissed a little, but we never..."

"More than friends but not exactly lovers." Vivian placed her index finger under her lower lip and looked up at the ceiling. "Dub was handsome but that is not what drew you to him. It was not his looks. So, what was it then?" Vivian's eyes moved from the ceiling and settled on Katherine.

"He was kind. He was understanding. He had a..." Katherine struggled with words, wanting to move on.

"A good spirit, maybe." Vivian suggested.

"Yes," Katherine agreed. "He had a good spirit."

Vivian smiled knowingly. "And now we are getting somewhere. He had a good spirit and that is why you fell for him."

Katherine did not feel like they were getting anywhere. "I guess you could say that."

"And would you say he still has a good spirit?" Vivian leaned back into the corner of the couch.

Katherine's brow scrunched above her nose. "I don't know. He can be a real pain in the... I mean he tries to act tough and uncaring but under it all I still see... a good spirit."

A smile spread across Vivian's face. "So you fell for him because he had a good spirit. And I'm willing to bet that he fell for you because down under that don't-mess-with-me façade you show the world, he saw the good spirit in you."

Katherine shrugged. "Okay, but I still don't see where this is going."

"We've just taken the first bite of the elephant." Vivian held up her hand and used it to demonstrate a bite being chewed. "We're ready to swallow it now. Your love for Dub is not based on a physical attraction. It is a spiritual love."

"What?" Katherine nearly squealed it came out so quickly. "I am not in love with Dub."

Vivian chuckled. "I cannot help you if you will not swallow this first bite. So many of us have been trained to believe that to be in love with someone there has to be a physical attraction and while that may be what starts most relationships, it is not real love. Real love happens when two spirits connect. All the touching, all the sex in the world, will never be as strong as a spiritual connection. And my child, that is what you are fighting against. Not only are you in love with Dub but you also love Dub. And to have both is something rare."

"But I do not even like him most of the time." Katherine continued to argue.

Vivian waved a finger in the air between them. "Love and

like are not the same. You can love someone and not like the way they act or what they are doing. On the other hand, you can like everything about someone, but for whatever reason it does not translate into love."

Katherine opened her mouth but every argument that came to her mind was a lie she could not voice. She did not want to be in love with Dub. She did not want to love Dub.

"He hurt me when he left." She could feel the old pain and tried to tap into it. "And now he has left again."

"Love is strong, my child," Vivian spoke softly. "It is so strong that even when we hide it away beneath hurt and pain, eventually it will rise to the surface. And I believe that is what is happening to you now."

"So, what?" Katherine wanted to run, wanted to scream. "So, what if I loved him? So, what if I have loved him all my life? So, what…?"

Her own words registered and as hard as she tried, she could not deny them. She had loved him through the hurt. Through the years. Through her failed marriage. The anger she had felt six months ago when she heard he was back in town was because she loved him. It made no sense, and it made all the sense in the world. She loved Dub Taylor.

As the tears began to fall, Vivian sat up and pulled Katherine's head into her shoulder. "I do love him but what do I do now?" Katherine asked between sobs.

"Oh, my child." Vivian rubbed her back. "Let that first bite settle for a bit and then we will discuss what to do about Dub and his land."

CHAPTER 30

Dub had just finished dressing Wednesday morning when there was a sharp rap on his door. "Mr. Taylor?"

The voice was Darion's he thought, but it sounded as if he was out of breath and very excited about something. Dub crossed to the door quickly and opened it. "What is it, Darion?"

"Mr. Taylor," Darion tried to talk and catch his breath at the same time, "There is a woman at the front desk who is insisting she be told where you are."

Dub's mind raced. The only woman who would come looking for him would be Kat, but it was not in her nature to chase after a man. If it had been, she would have tried harder when they were younger. He stepped into the hallway and pointed for Darion to lead the way.

As they turned the corner, Dub saw Katherine with one hand on her hip and the index finger of her other hand pointing at the receptionist. The middle-aged woman across the counter from Katherine was on her feet, arms across her chest, shaking her head. Dub tried to remember her name and could not.

"Darion, what's the receptionist's name?" he asked as they got closer.

"Tina," Darion replied quickly.

"Tina, it's okay, I know her." Dub had to raise his voice to be heard over Katherine.

Both women turned to look at him. Tina shrugged but did not look happy. Katherine reached down and picked up a package before turning back to face him. "Dub Taylor we need to talk."

"Okay." Dub was not sure what else he should say.

Tina sat back down in the rolling chair behind the desk and picked up a pen and paper. Dub could tell she was only acting like she was ignoring them. Darion made no such show. He stood beside Dub as if he was a bodyguard ready to intervene. Dub mentally smiled at the thought of what would happen if his self-appointed protection got in the way of the little woman in front of them.

"Well, don't you have a room or something?" Katherine stamped her foot.

Dub turned sideways, bent slightly at the waist, and motioned down the hallway. "Right this way, my lady."

As Katherine stormed past, Darion looked down at Dub. "You gonna be okay, Mr. Taylor?"

"I think I can handle this." He slapped the big man on the shoulder. "But if you hear furniture breaking, send in the troops."

Katherine was passing his door when he caught up to her. "It's this one, Kat." He opened the door and followed her inside.

Two steps into the room, she stopped. The room was too small for Dub to move past her. "Kat, what are you doing here?"

Instead of answering, Katherine walked to the room's only chair and set the package in it. Another couple of steps and she opened his bathroom door before turning to look at him.

"I had a talk with Mason, your lawyer," she was not yelling but there was an undertone of anger and something he could not quite place in her tone. "I was so angry with you… so angry, but then I went to visit Vivian. I don't like you very much right now, Dub Taylor."

Twice in less than five minutes she had used both of his names. He felt like he should say something, maybe make a joke about her not liking him at all, but before he could form the thought into a sentence, she continued, "It's spiritual. That's what Vivian said. It was very confusing until it all made sense. Vivian helped me see it."

"Kat, you're not making any sense," Dub started towards her.

She threw up her hand and pointed a finger at him. "Don't... You stay right there. I'm not ready yet. I need to be mad at you a little longer."

Dub stopped. "Not ready for what?" Something inside him screamed that he did not want to know the answer to the question, but it slipped out before it completely registered.

"Forty years, Dub, forty years! That is how long I was mad at you," Katherine punctuated her words by shaking her finger at him repeatedly. "That is how long it was hidden down deep in my soul. It was covered up by hurt and pain for forty years. It is why I never really loved my husband. It is why I have felt lost all these years."

"What in the world are you talking about, Kat?" Dub had begun to wonder if there was something he had forgotten.

Katherine walked to the bed and sat down on it. She stared at the floor for what seemed like forever, but was not more than a minute or two. It took all of Dub's mental power not to disobey her and cross to her. When she looked back up at him, he could see tears in her eyes. "Dub Taylor, I'm in love with you. I fell in love with you when we were kids and I never stopped loving you. I love you."

Her words cut him to his very soul. His legs threatened to drop him in the floor. He felt like he needed to sit down.

"Don't say that." It was his voice, but it felt like someone else was using it. "You cannot love me. It's too late. You cannot."

Her tears continued to flow. "I can say whatever I want to. You don't get to tell me what I can and cannot say any more than you can tell me who I can love. And I love you."

Dub could not wait any longer for her permission. He crossed the room, sat down on the bed beside her, and pulled her into his arms. "It is too late," he whispered as he held her close.

"It's never too late," she whispered back. "You told me that. You told me to remember it."

"This is not what I meant." The lump in his throat threatened to choke him.

"Tell me you don't love me, and I'll leave." She pushed away from him and forced him to look into her eyes.

His mind screamed it was too late. Everything about him shouted time was too short. He formed the words in his mind, but his heart betrayed him. "I don't... I don't... I can't... I can't say it, Kat. I have loved you for so long, but it's too late. It will not be long until I don't even remember my own name."

"I don't care," Dub could see the defiance in her eyes. "I'll take whatever I can get. Every minute, every second, whatever I can get, I want them. I, we, have wasted so much time, I won't waste anymore."

"I can't even begin to imagine how this would work." he swallowed hard, but the lump refused to budge.

"You could come live with me." Katherine offered. The sincerity in her words rang true.

Dub shook his head but did not speak.

"Why not?" Katherine pled, "I can take care of you."

His lip began to quiver, and he no longer had the ability or will to hold back his emotions. Through the tears, he spoke, "You don't want to watch what is going to happen to me."

"I do." She took his hands in hers.

"I don't want you to." He leaned his forehead against hers. "Kat, I can't bear the thought of you watching my mind go. There will come a day when I won't know who you are, and I don't want that for you."

"I don't care," she whispered as she pressed her forehead harder into his, "and I'm not leaving until we figure this out."

An hour later, Katherine had still not been able to sway him into returning to Tishomingo. Beyond frustrated, she stood up and retrieved the package from the chair where she had placed it.

"Vivian and Brother Jerry told me there was nothing I could say that would change your mind about coming back," She said as she handed it to Dub. "I guess they were right."

Dub took the package. "I'm sorry Kat."

"Go ahead and open it." She sat down in the chair.

With care, he took the paper wrapping off and sat and stared at the finished painting of him and Katherine standing on the tailgate of his dad's truck. He looked at her and started to speak but she cut him off. "Don't you even think about refusing that. I painted it for you, and Dub Taylor, you will hang it in the room and look at it every damn day. And it will remind you every minute that I can't be here of how much I love you. Do you understand me?"

"Yes, my lady." Katherine watched him smile and knew he was fighting back tears.

"Pick a day of the week." She stood and took the painting from him and began to move it around the room trying to decide the best place to hang it.

"What for?" She heard him say from behind her.

"It will be the day I come to see you every week." She walked to the wall across from the foot of his bed. "I may come on other days, but I will always be here on whatever day you pick."

"What days are best for you?" he asked as she gauged the center of his bed while holding the painting against the wall.

She thought about it for a moment, "Not Wednesday, that's church night. And not Sundays, Jenn usually comes out to the house for most of the day."

"Thursday?" His eyes met hers.

"Thursday, it is." Katherine smiled. "Now go find someone who can help us hang this painting."

Dub found Darion visiting with Tina and explained what was needed. In short order, a set of plastic wall hangers were retrieved from a utility closet and Dub and Darion returned to Dub's room.

"Kat, this is Darion." Dub made the introductions as soon as the door shut, "Darion this is Kat."

"Nice to meet you, Miz Kat." Darion nodded.

"Miz Kat. I like the sound of that." Katherine smiled at the big man. "It's very nice to meet you as well, Mr. Darion."

Darion grinned and Dub laughed.

"Mr. Darion, I want to tell you something about this man here." Katherine pointed her chin in his direction. "He is the biggest jackass I've ever met. He is stubborn and hardheaded. I'd even go as far as to say he is the biggest pain in the ass you are ever likely to run into, but I love him. And Mr. Darion, since he refused to let me take him home with me, I want your word that you will take very good care of him."

Darion bowed low at the waist and as he rose, smiled. "Miz Kat, you have my word."

"Good, now let's get this painting hung."

CHAPTER 31

For the next three years, seven months, and two weeks, Katherine made the trip from Tishomingo to Sulphur every Thursday without fail. Slowly the disease took Dub's memory and in the winter of the second year, he no longer remembered who Katherine was and spent most of their visits watching her with a blank stare as she read from the Bible to him.

Mr. Darion, as Katherine had affectionately named Dub's favorite person at the center, kept her apprised of weekly changes in Dub's behavior, eating habits, and anything he felt she would want to know. Even after Dub lost the ability to communicate, Darion let her know that every Thursday morning, Dub would become more animated. Darion swore that somewhere deep within Mr. Taylor's subconscious, he knew Miz Kat was going to visit.

"Miz Kat," Darion stopped her on her way into the center in spring of the third year, "I have never seen love as strong as what you and Mr. Taylor share. Yesterday, I went into the room, and he was staring at that picture you made me hang on the wall the first time we met. At least, I thought he was staring at it, so I took it down and took it over to him. When I asked him if he remembered who gave it to him, he touched your name where you signed it and his eyes lit up."

It took Katherine most of the first year after Dub moved to Sulphur to decide what to do with his family's home and land.

During that time, she continued to attend services and teach Sunday school at the All Faith Christian Church where her friendship with Judi grew. At the end of the semester that year, Judi's roommates all left, and she could not afford to rent the house by herself. Katherine offered Judi one of her upstairs rooms. Judi would not accept the offer without paying for it, and so after some serious negotiations, a price was set, and Judi moved in. When the next fall semester began, she rented out the other rooms to three young college girls. Two of the students were nursing friends of Judi's and the third was Jim and Faith Lovett's niece who was in the veterinarian nursing program.

Jenn's visits became more and more frequent and one evening when Jenn and her mother and Katherine's little flock of renters all gathered around the kitchen bar to gorge themselves on the pizza Jenn had brought from town, Katherine turned to her daughter. "You know Jenn, you're out here more than you're at that little apartment you rent in town anymore."

Jenn looked at her mother and the others stopped talking to listen. "I was thinking it's a shame for you to pay rent when you could just move into the downstairs guest room and save your money."

Amidst the squeals and pleas to accept from the other girls, Jenn agreed to think about it. Two months later she moved into the guest room.

The Friday after Katherine's first visit to the Veteran's Center, she walked into Mason's office and formally accepted the terms of Dub's agreement. The paperwork was signed, and she took possession of the land and Dub's truck. She sold her car the following week and although Mason was told that she always referred to it as Dub's truck, she drove it proudly.

A little over a year later, Katherine surprised Mason when she walked into his office and sat down. Confused, he flipped open his appointment book. "I'm sorry, Mrs. Williams, I…"

"I don't have an appointment, Mason." Katherine stopped him. "And I would very much like it if you just called me Kat."

"But..." He could tell by the look on her face that while it had seemed like a request, it was not. "Yes, ma'am, Kat. What can I do for you today?"

"I would like to turn Dub's land into a wildlife rescue and sanctuary. I want to hire you to help me with the legal aspect of setting it up." Katherine took a checkbook from her purse as she spoke. "How much do you need as a retainer?"

Mason's jaw dropped. He sat not knowing what to say or how to react. When Katherine looked up, he closed his mouth and somehow managed, "Why me?"

Pen posed to write, Katherine shrugged. "For a couple of reasons. First, Dub explained to me that you are the hardest working lawyer in town. He said other attorneys were more popular, but they would not go the extra mile like you would. Add to that the fact that I was a total bitch to you for no other reason than I could be and instead of telling Dub to find someone else, you stuck it out. I want someone who is going to help me even if the going gets rough."

Mason mulled over what he had just heard before speaking. "In that case, Kat, my usual retainer is five hundred dollars."

He watched her write the check, tear it out, and offer it to him across the desk. Leaning forward, he took it from her, half expecting to see the word "Gotcha" written across the middle of it. A quick look told him it was indeed made out to him and in the right amount. He laid it beside his appointment book and took out a legal pad.

For the next half-hour, Katherine explained her plans and he took notes. She had a number of questions, most of them he knew the answers to, but a couple he had to tell her he would research and get back to her on. When they were both satisfied that there was nothing more that needed to be discussed, Katherine stood up and stuck out her hand.

He rose and took it. As they shook hands, Katherine smiled.

"Mr. Boyd, I owe you an apology. The way I have treated you in the past was unacceptable. I hope you can find it in your heart to forgive me and I hope that you will think of yourself not only as my lawyer but my friend. I am truly sorry."

Before he could respond, Katherine released his hand, and without looking back crossed to the door and let herself out. He stood and stared at the door and wondered if the last hour had not been a figment of his imagination. His eyes moved from the door to his desk and settled on the check laying there, five hundred dollars made out to him from Katherine Williams and on the memo line the word retainer.

Mason stepped around the edge of his desk and walked over to the file cabinet. He took the half full bottle of bourbon and glass out. With one final look at the check, he walked down the hall to the bathroom. Standing in front of the mirror, he poured two fingers of the amber liquid into the glass and held it out towards his reflection. "This one is for you Dub Taylor. How you managed it, the Good Lord only knows." And he turned the glass upside down and poured the bourbon into the sink. As it made its way down the drain, Mason looked to the ceiling. *When You give a sign, You really give a sign*, he thought as he turned the bottle up over the sink and listened to the sound of it glugging. When the last of the bourbon had vanished, he tossed the empty glass and bottle into the metal trashcan just inside the bathroom door.

Dub's words, *You are stronger than you think you are*, ran through his mind as he walked back into his office and sat down.

On the third Tuesday after the New Year, Katherine stood in front of her easel. She had just finished signing her latest painting with her usual KAT signature when her cellphone rang. The screen indicated it was Mason Boyd calling.

Katherine wiped the paint from her index finger, tapped the accept icon and then the speaker, "Good afternoon, Mason."

"Kat, I'm afraid I have some bad news," his voice broke, and it took him a second before he continued. "I got a call from Sulphur. Dub has passed."

She looked from the phone to the painting and then to the photograph she had used to create it. In the month before Dub forgot who she was, Darion had snapped the picture of Dub dancing with her in the hallway at the center.

"Thank you for calling." Katherine looked at the phone as she spoke, "I will be at your office in the morning to help with the final arrangements. What is a good time?"

She heard Mason sniffle, then say, "Eight o'clock if that's not too early."

"I'll see you then." She had to work hard to keep her voice from breaking. "Mason, we will get through this, I promise you we will."

When he did not respond, she gently touched the red circle on her phone and ended the call. For several seconds, she stood and stared at the painting in front of her, letting her memory take her back to the day it was taken. She could feel the touch of his hand on her waist as he guided her up and down the hallway. Closing her eyes, she could hear the song he was singing and smell his cologne. When the song ended, she opened her eyes and the strength that had been holding her upright vanished. She held the edge of the table for support and lowered herself onto the floor. Once there Katherine placed both hands over her face and sobbed.

CHAPTER 32

Katherine arrived at the cemetery early on the day of the funeral. She and Mason had spent the days between the phone call and that Saturday explaining to the pastors and members of each of the churches Dub had attended that he had given very specific dos and don'ts, and a graveside service was all he wanted.

As Katherine opened the door of Dub's truck and stepped down, the cold January wind hit her, pressing her long denim skirt against her legs. The folks from the funeral home had everything set up and ready. Clutching her Bible to her chest, Katherine made her way to the blue tent beside the grave.

"Mrs. Williams, I believe everything is as you and Mr. Boyd requested," the funeral director's words were soft and reassuring. "Is there anything else you need from me?"

"I do not believe so." She sat down in one of the folding chairs under the tent. "I just wanted a minute before Dub got here."

"I understand." The director took a step away before stopping. "Do you have an idea of how many people will be attending?"

"Not really." Katherine looked up at him. "I think only a few and the color guard."

"I see." He bowed his head. "I'll be close if you need anything."

Katherine watched him walk away before opening her Bible. She had used the picture of her and Dub dancing as a bookmark and now she sat looking at it. Somehow holding it in her hands made her feel less alone.

The crunch of gravel as a vehicle approached caused Katherine to look up. It was a white van from the Veteran's Center. It pulled to a stop a short distance away and Darion stepped out and started towards her. She met him at the edge of the tent and gave him a hug.

The big man spoke softly, "Miz Kat, I'm so sorry."

Another vehicle approaching caused the two to turn around. Jenn pulled to a stop behind Darion's van, stepped out, and walked to her mother's side.

"Jenn this is Mr. Darion," Katherine started introductions, then saw that the hearse had rounded the far bend and was slowly making its way toward them. Behind it a line of vehicles stretched out. Katherine's eyes moved along each car and truck searching for the end. Before she could find the end, the director stepped to her side. "Ma'am, there are more than a few."

"Yes, I believe you are right," Katherine agreed with a smile.

In the twenty minutes that followed, Katherine with Jenn beside her shook more hands, received more condolences, and was hugged more times than she could count. Members from all five of the churches Dub had attended had shown up, as well as many people from the community. Some of them explained how they knew Dub, but most did not.

Katherine did not know when Mason had arrived but at the appointed time, he along with five of Dub's friends chosen as pallbearer's removed the flag-draped casket from the hearse. As bagpipes played "Amazing Grace", they made their way to the gravesite and lowered the casket onto the catafalque.

Mason stepped back and introduced Brother Jerry who led them in the Lord's Prayer. When the prayer was over, Katherine took a seat along with Jenn and five of the pallbearer's wives. Taps was played, the twenty-one-gun salute was fired, and the bagpiper walked away playing a song Katherine did not know the name of before the color guard came forward.

The flag was removed from Dub's casket and folded with

care before being presented to Katherine. She had sworn to herself that she would not cry. When the soldier kneeled in front of her, placed the flag in her hands, and thanked her for Dub's service to his country, she wept.

"Brother Jerry will lead us in a closing prayer and then Katherine has something she needs to read and perhaps a few words to say." She heard Mason's voice as Faith handed her a box of tissues.

At the end of Brother Jerry's prayer, Katherine stood up, wiped her eyes once more, and took a single sheet of paper out of the front of her Bible. "Almost four years ago, I entered into an agreement with Dub Taylor, who at the time I could not stand." Behind her one of the pallbearers snickered. She was not sure but if she had been a betting woman, she would have put her money on Jim Lovett.

"The contract I entered into was for the property which Dub's family owned and lived on. The price he set for the acreage was seven dates. The last stipulation of our deal was that I read what is written on this paper." Katherine held up the paper and then began, "We are here today to lay to rest the body of Dub Garrett Taylor. I am here to fulfill an agreement I made to procure a parcel of land. I have agreed to speak over this dead man as the fulfillment of our seventh date."

As the tears rolled down her cheeks, she placed the paper back in the front of her Bible and looked at the people around her. "A lot of you I don't know, but if you are here, it is my guess that you knew Dub. And if you knew Dub, you know he was one of a kind. I would like to say that Dub is laughing at me from his mansion in Heaven. But Dub would have me remind you that it is only the Good Lord who makes the decision of our eternal home and words after one's death do not sway the Almighty. Or in Dub's own words—'Kat don't you dare try to preach me into Heaven. If'n the Lord's willing to forgive my sins, if He's accepted my repentance, then I'm in, and if'n He cain't then it's my own durn fault for my hellish ways here on earth'."

She stopped and wiped tears away. "I don't know about his hellish ways. I know how stubborn he could be, and I am so thankful for that stubbornness because it saved me. It would take me too much time to explain how, so I'll just say Dub Taylor saved me, and we'll leave it at that."

Katherine returned to her seat and the crowd began to slowly dwindle. Over the years she had grown close to the wives she had met at Dub's makeshift drive-in movie night. The six of them and Jenn visited beside Dub's casket. The five men from that night, who had served as pallbearers reminisced behind them. Mason approached with the funeral director once everyone had left.

"Kat, I'm going now." Mason looked down at her. "But if you need anything give me a call."

"Thank you so much, Mason." She reached out and squeezed his hand.

One by one the others drifted off until it was just her and Jenn.

"Are you about ready?" Jenn wrapped an arm around her shoulders.

"Yes, but I'd like a minute alone with him." Katherine patted Jenn's hand.

"I'll wait in the car and follow you home when you're ready." She gave Katherine a hug before standing up and walking away.

Katherine brushed at the top of the flag in her lap and collected her thoughts. She looked up and forced a smile, "Dub Taylor, you were a jackass. My favorite jackass and I'm going to miss you." The smile faded as she began to cry once more. "I have never hated anyone as much as I hated you. And I don't need to tell you that I have never loved anyone the way I loved you. You once told me that it was never too late and then you went and made me believe it. I don't know what my future holds but I know that as long as I live, I will hold your memory close to me and I will love you forever."

CHAPTER 33

Four months later at the beginning of May, Katherine sat behind her desk in the Dub Taylor Memorial Wildlife Rescue and Sanctuary. She had converted Dub's house into the welcome center and the living room served as her office. It had taken two years for Mason to get all the legal documents in order and another six months to renovate the residence and make the upgrades to the old barn but now it was ready for business.

The door opened and Katherine looked up to see a young couple looking around, "Can I help you?" she asked.

"I'll wait outside," the young man placed his hand on the girl's back before retreating through the door.

"I'm here about the job in the paper." She stepped forward. "Has the position been filled?"

Katherine stood up and offered her a hand. "It has not. I'm Kat, and you are?"

"Gentry Banks," she smiled nervously as she took Katherine's hand, "I would like to apply for it then, Mrs. Taylor."

Katherine smiled at the Mrs. Taylor but did not correct her. "Have a seat."

Gentry sat on the edge of one of the two chairs in front of Katherine's desk with her hands clasped in her lap. Katherine asked her several questions and made a couple of notations on a notepad, but she had already decided she liked Gentry and was going to give her the position.

"Do you have any questions for me, Gentry?" Katherine laid the pen with which she writing aside.

212

Gentry looked past her. "Are those your kids?" she asked pointing at the painting Katherine had hung on the wall behind her desk.

She did not bother to turn around. "No, that is me and Mr. Taylor when we were kids." Katherine felt the glow deep inside even before the smile spread across her face.

"I see." Gentry nodded. "I would really like this job. I love to work with animals."

"To be honest with you," Katherine leaned forward, "I have three positions to fill but I have never had to hire someone, so I have no idea what I'm doing."

"Oh." Gentry's head lowered.

"But I like you." Katherine watched as she looked back up and could see the hope in her eyes. "So, you're hired."

Gentry clapped her hands. "Oh, thank you, Mrs. Taylor."

Katherine held up her hands. "The first rule if you are going to work for me is that you call me Kat."

"Got it." Gentry smiled.

"Now, does your boyfriend have a job?" Katherine asked.

Gentry looked confused. "I don't have a boyfriend."

Katherine pointed to the door. "Who was the young man that came in with you?"

"Oh, that's Sam." Gentry glanced over her shoulder and then quickly back at Katherine. "My cars in the shop but it will be out tomorrow. Sam offered to give me a ride out here, but he's just a friend."

Katherine shook her head and smiled. "I had a friend once that looked at me like Sam looks at you. If you're smart you will latch on to him and never let him out of your sight. I didn't and... well, how would you feel about me offering Sam a job?"

DEAR READER,

First and foremost, I want to say *Thank You* to **You**. Without you, the reader, books are simply marks on paper. Thanks to you the words on the pages of this novel are no longer just random scribbling they are the shared story they were meant to be.

I cannot vouch for other writers but for me the idea for a story is often generated by something I see or hear, and this one was no different. With that said, I want to thank Kathy Fuss for sharing a story from our childhood that sparked the thoughts that led to this book. Thank You, Kathy.

As with any story, movement from an idea to the reality of a book, takes a number of special people. With that in mind, I would like to thank my mom and dad, who are the major driving forces behind my writing. A huge *Thank You*, to my developmental editors, Joani Hartin and Denise Sanders, without your help with commas and quotation marks, I would truly be lost. And without my formatter, Judi Fennell, there is no telling what pages within these covers would look like, so Thank You, Judi.

In addition, I would like to thank the three ladies that did a final read of this book before it went live. Mrs. Lindsey Ramon, Mrs. Kayla Arnold, and Mrs. Tammara Cook, thanks to each of you for your help in getting this book ready for the readers. You are greatly appreciated.

Until next time,
Charles Lemar Brown

215

ABOUT THE AUTHOR

Charles Lemar Brown is a retired high school science teacher, who now spends much of his time writing and traveling. In addition to this work, he has also published two novels, *The Road to Nowhere, The Neon Church Journal*, as well as a book of short stories entitled *Raised Redneck, Vol. 1*. He is also an avid photographer whose photographs have been sold around the world. He lives  in rural Love County, Oklahoma, where he enjoys spending time with his seven children and nineteen grandchildren. Left alone too long, he is likely to be found making TikTok's, working out in his home gym, or kicked back with his cat, Tilee, watching whatever football game he can find on the television. His favorite quote is—what doesn't kill you makes you stronger and I ain't dead yet.

Made in the USA
Monee, IL
20 September 2023

43083713R00125